FINDING A WIFE
FOR TANNER

Golden Gate Romance Series, Book Three

BARBARA MCMAHON

Finding a Wife For Tanner
Copyright © 2022 Barbara McMahon
All Rights Reserved

1

Tanner Wright stood at the side of the crowded room letting the conversations swirl around him. He took a sip of champagne. Only the best for this crowd. He looked across the room where Marie DuPont held court. She purported to be his date for the evening, not that she'd spent much time with him, or anyone else for that matter. Marie liked to flit and flirt and show off before as many people as possible.

He studied her dispassionately from across the room. Her sleek blond hair was cut short in a sophisticated style that emphasized her high cheekbones and her almond-shaped cat's eyes. The slinky black gown she wore highlighted her best features, the curves that declared her all woman.

But she laughed rather shrilly, and seemed to constantly be switching empty glasses for full ones. He adjusted the sleeve of his tuxedo and noted the time. A stunning woman, and she knew it. But he didn't care. She wasn't what he sought, after all. A shame, really. On the surface, she met all his requirements.

"Tanner?"

He looked around and smiled. Sean Murphy was a longtime friend. Tanner suspected he'd be here tonight.

"Sean, good to see you."

"I admit I'm surprised to see you here. This isn't the kind of event you usually attend."

"I'm escorting Marie DuPont," Tanner murmured.

At Sean's grimace, Tanner lifted an eyebrow.

"Something wrong?"

Sean shook his head. "Marie isn't exactly on my top-ten list, that's all."

He glanced across the room to the tall blonde, his expression one of blatant disapproval.

"Ah, and what list does she make?" Tanner asked.

"Last person I'd wanted to be stranded on a desert island with," Sean replied without hesitation. "I didn't know you knew her."

"A recent introduction."

"Mmm."

Sean looked back at his friend.

"Are these charity events always so crowded?" Tanner asked as he faced the room again, taking in the diamonds and sapphires that glittered, the designer gowns that offered splashes of vibrant color contrasting so sharply with the black tuxedos.

The ballroom at the St. Francis Hotel seemed to overflow. Standing well over six feet gave him an advantage when studying the crowd. Tanner was used to taking advantage whatever the circumstances.

"If you'd come to some of them more often, you'd know that they are. Everyone likes to be seen at these things. It's considered an event, and once here you are supposed to try to donate more than the next man. But only if you're sure everyone knows exactly the amount on your check," Sean said.

"You're getting cynical in your old age, Sean."

Tanner scanned the room again, recognizing acquainttances and business associates. He didn't count the majority of people here his friends. In fact, Sean was probably the only true friend he had in the room. The two of them went back a long time.

"If so, I'm only catching up with you. What's the real deal, Tanner? Why are you here tonight and with Marie DuPont of all people?" Sean asked after a moment. "I've never known you to socialize at an event like this. Is it business?"

Tanner shrugged. "Just looking."

"For what?"

Tanner hesitated, then spoke slowly. He didn't often share his personal plans or ambitions with anyone. But Sean had known him when he was the kid from the wrong side of the tracks, working two part-time jobs and studying constantly to keep his grades up for his scholarship at Stanford University.

Sean had been born with a silver spoon—an entire service—in his mouth. Yet the two of them, oddly enough, had become friends that first day at Stanford.

"Looking for a wife," Tanner said, turning to catch his friend's reaction.

Sean didn't disappoint him. He stared in stunned surprise.

"A wife? I thought you didn't believe in love and all that stuff."

"You're correct, I don't. What does that have to do with anything?" Tanner asked impatiently. "Are you going to tell me there are no women out there who would take me on as a husband because I don't love them?"

"Half the women in the city would take you on with your money and looks. You know that. But that kind of a relationship would give you the short end of the stick."

"Not if that's all I want."

"And what do you want, exactly?"

"Someone to start a family with and provide what I don't have now."

"Marie DuPont?" Sean scoffed.

"Let's just say she's in the running."

"Forget it, Tanner, she's not the one for you."

"No?"

"Not Marie. What are you looking for--entrée into the highest of old San Francisco's society? Money? Family? Roots?"

"Breeding," Tanner said softly, an edge to his voice.

Sean scanned the crowded ballroom, returned his gaze to his friend.

"Look, I know where you're coming from, with your background and all. But I think you're plumb crazy. You don't marry some woman just for breeding."

"You do if you want to make sure your kids never have the problems I had as a child."

"Get real, Tanner, with your fortune, no kid of yours is ever going to come close to the life you had."

"I want more than what money can buy. I want him to have the right family, the right connections, go to the right schools."

Not have to claw and scratch his way to the top like his father, he thought. His son would start out with everything in his favor. And Tanner meant to see his son had all the advantages—including a father while he was growing up.

He wasn't getting any younger. Time to find a wife and start his family.

"Marie drinks. Her mother's a lush and her father's on the verge of bankruptcy. They give a good show, but they aren't in the top echelons of society. You've been in that ivory business tower of yours too long if you think they are. Time to mingle and get to know these people before doing something so entangling as marriage. If it doesn't work, you'll be stuck with a ton of alimony."

"I don't plan to enter into marriage thinking it's going to end," Tanner said calmly.

"Then you better be darn sure you get what you want first time."

"I agree."

Sean ran his fingers through his hair in frustration.

"Tanner, you aren't going to rush into this, are you?"

"I'll be thirty-six on my next birthday, I hardly think I'm rushing into anything. I could be close to forty by the time a baby arrives. I'd like to be young enough to enjoy him."

"You can't run after any old woman and marry her."

"I'm not just running after any old woman, I'm very particular in what I want."

"You may be some hot-shot financial whiz, but when it comes to knowing what's what in San Francisco society, you're a babe in the woods. You haven't made enough contacts to know who's worth cultivating and whom you should avoid. Business is one thing, this is different," Sean protested.

"I'm sure I can manage," Tanner said stiffly.

"What you need is someone who can let you know about these people," Sean said impulsively. "Someone who knows the backgrounds, the skeletons in the closets and isn't afraid to share that information."

Tanner gave his friend a sardonic smile, and shook his head.

"Planning to vet my choices?" he asked.

"I don't know, maybe. You don't know these people like I do. You don't know who's in financial difficulty and who is not quite top drawer. I've been around them all my life. I know the inside gossip."

"A lot of which I can find out. Just like I discover which stocks have the best prospective, which bonds are the most lucrative, which start-up ventures hold the most promise."

"Tanner, darling."

The tall, sleek woman they'd been discussing moments before drifted over to him and slid her arm possessively into the crook of his.

Pouting artfully, she batted her eyes at Sean before gazing adoringly up at Tanner.

"I've had enough of this party, darling. Why don't we go and have one of our own?"

"If you are tired of being here, we can leave," he said politely.

There'd be no private party. He'd had enough and Sean was right. Marie wasn't the woman he wanted to be the mother of his son.

"Good to see you again, Sean. Call and set up lunch sometime," Tanner said, covering Marie's hand with his own.

He noticed the glances people threw his way, the speculation that ran rampant. When Marie preened a bit, he knew she'd seen it, as well, and apparently jumped to the same conclusion as the others.

But he hadn't come this far in life to be caught in any snare not of his own choosing.

"Monday," Sean said. "I'll be by your office late Monday morning and we'll go to lunch then."

Tanner escorted the lovely Marie home. She was not pleased at the abrupt ending to their evening, but Tanner didn't really care. His time was too valuable to waste with someone unsuitable.

"Good night, Marie."

He prepared to leave her at her door.

"Call me, Tanner," she said, her eyes glittering in suppressed frustration.

He smiled, but didn't commit.

"Mr. Murphy is here."

Rachel's efficient voice announced Sean's arrival over the intercom Monday at noon.

Tanner regretted on Sunday that he'd told Sean his plans. He didn't want a lecture during lunch or to listen to any of Sean's schemes to choose the right wife. Sean was one of the few people in the world who couldn't be intimidated by Tanner.

Sometimes there was a downside to long-term friends.

Besides, he'd made up his mind. Examining all the aspects of marriage, he'd determined that choosing a suitable bride from one of the top families in San Francisco would insure the best for any children and wouldn't hurt current business ventures.

Tanner was pragmatic and goal oriented. He knew his money and success in the market would be a strong complement to the breeding and background of his future wife. A perfect blending of assets to form a strong bond.

"Send him in."

Tanner remained another moment by the large window, gazing over the other high-rise office buildings comprising San Francisco's financial district. Hearing the click at the door, he moved from the window and crossed the room as Sean entered.

They gripped hands in greeting.

"I've got it," Sean said.

"What?" Tanner asked, shrugging into his suit jacket. "Not the flu, I hope?"

"No, the solution to your problem. To both our problems, as a matter of fact."

"I didn't know we both had a problem," Tanner said as they left for lunch.

They walked down the street to the small bar and grill on the corner of Montgomery. The restaurant was crowded, but the hostess knew Tanner by sight and reputation and quickly found a secluded table. Once their orders had been given, Sean sat back, raised his water glass in a mock toast and nodded.

"I've got the perfect solution to your problem. And in exchange, you can help me out with mine."

Tanner raised an eyebrow.

"Indeed. And is that a goal of mine, helping you out?"

Sean shook his head, laughing softly.

"Probably not, but it'll do you good once in a while to help a friend."

"Especially when I have so few of them."

"You'd have more than you ever wanted if you'd let

anyone close to you," Sean fired back bluntly.

"My life's going just how I want it," Tanner replied.

Knowing when to back off, Sean nodded, then continued, "Right. That's why you want to get married."

"Haven't you thought about it?" Tanner asked.

Sean was the same age. Didn't he also long for a family, for a new generation to leave behind when his time was up?

"Of course. When Betsy was alive, I thought we'd marry and have a slough full of kids. I haven't met anyone I've loved as much since she died."

Tanner said nothing. He remembered how his friend had loved Betsy Springer. Her death had hit him hard.

"But we're not talking about me, my friend, we're talking about you and your scheme to marry into some highfalutin society family who can trace its roots back to the gold rush. I have a plan," Sean said.

"You have the perfect solution to finding the right woman?" Tanner asked skeptically.

"Sunny," Sean said proudly.

"Sunny?" Tanner asked. Was the word supposed to mean something to him?

"My cousin Sunny. She can introduce you to the right people, give you some background on the women themselves, match you up with the perfect mate."

"You expect your cousin to play matchmaker?" Tanner asked slowly, his eyes narrowing as he studied Sean across the table. He didn't even know the woman.

"Sort of."

"Sort of." Tanner continued to stare at his friend. "How does this help you?"

Sean smoothed his tie, an obvious nervous gesture.

"Hear me out, Tanner. I figure this could go both ways, she'll help you and you can help her. And helping her in this case would help me."

Sean cleared his throat.

Tanner narrowed his eyes.

"Spill it all, Sean."

"Sunny's in a bit of a bind. And you're the cause."

"I don't even know a Sunny."

"No, but Brad Peterson does."

"Ah, I begin to get the picture." Tanner nodded, his expression forbidding. "Let me guess. This Sunny persuaded Brad to invest in some wild business scheme and now she can't pay the return."

"Something like that, only her business isn't so wild. I think she needs a bit of help getting the place off the ground. But since Brad left—"

"Was fired, you mean? He had no sense of business. We'd be flat busted if he'd continued," Tanner interjected in a hard tone.

"Be that as it may, your company underwrote my cousin's new business. Now that Brad's gone, your new guy is pressing to call the loan. She can't make it. I don't want her to go under. Cut her some slack, give her a bit of time, that's all I'm asking. I think she can pull it off. I wouldn't ask if I didn't think so, you know that, Tanner."

Tanner studied his friend for a long moment.

"And in exchange for this bit of time, she'll find me a wife?"

Sean winced.

"Well, let's just say we can get her to introduce you to possible mates. Sunny can't really force anyone to go out with you or marry you. But she can introduce you to the kind of woman you are looking for—not someone like Marie DuPont."

"How much does this Sunny owe me?"

"A lot."

"You're worth a lot," Tanner murmured.

"Sunny needs help, but she's too stubborn and proud to accept it from the family. I thought this would make it a business deal—for both of you."

"Business deal? This isn't my idea of business, Sean."

"I don't know. The way you're going about looking for a wife isn't very romantic. In fact it smacks of business to me. Just think about it. That's all I'm asking. Sunny has a small shop, a bridal salon. She started it a couple of years ago and is barely making ends meet, yet I think she does good work, always seems busy. I think she needs someone to help on the business side. It's not as if you're going to lose anything by delaying on forcing her out. Give her a chance, and see if you can spot where she needs to tighten up or do something to turn the place around. It gives you a better shot at recapturing your capital, and with Sunny's help, you could end up with the best trophy bride San Francisco has to offer."

"I do not run shops," Tanner said distinctly.

"Of course not, who'd expect you to? It's a bridal shop, not something a man like you would be involved in. But you could look over her books, make sure she's doing things correctly. And then advise her where the business is weak and how to shore it up. That kind of thing. An afternoon's work at most."

"Do you know what I charge for that kind of service?" Tanner said ominously.

Sean grinned.

"A bundle. Sunny couldn't afford a minute of your time if she had to pay you for it. See, that's the beauty of my plan, she gives you something money can't even buy, introductions to all the right people and inside information on the prospective brides you couldn't get elsewhere."

Tanner shook his head.

"I think you're crazy."

"Give it some thought. I'll run it by Sunny and the two of you can take it from there," Sean said enthusiastically.

"And who exactly is Sunny?" Tanner asked.

He'd give it some thought, like four seconds, then tell Sean to keep his stupid ideas to himself in the future. Tanner didn't need help finding his own wife.

"Sunny is my cousin. Her mother is Mom's younger sister. When she was a girl, Sunny's mom ran off with a cop. They were in love."

Tanner took a sip of the white wine the waitress had delivered. He was growing a bit impatient with all Sean's love stories. Never having experienced that emotion, Tanner didn't give much credence to it. A purely business arrangement seemed much more likely to succeed over the long haul.

"So they got married and lived happily ever after," Tanner muttered dryly.

Sean nodded. "Until Uncle Will died. Killed by some druggie. He left them nothing. It was just the two of them, practically destitute."

"Didn't your aunt move back home?"

Sean shook his head.

"Nope, too proud. And too stubborn—same trend you'll find in Sunny. They stuck it out on their own, poor as church mice, from the way my mother tells it."

"So you want help for your poor-as-a-church-mouse cousin—"

"Hey, I'm not finished. Hold on and hear the rest. The part that makes Sunny the perfect solution for this problem."

Tanner glanced impatiently at his watch. Where was lunch? The service didn't usually take this long. He'd made a mistake in telling Sean about his search for a bride. Now he had to get through lunch and send the man on his way.

Once back in the office, he'd have Fielding check into the loan agreement for this Sunny's business.

"When Sunny was ten, Aunt Susan married Theo Quackenbush."

"Talk about old money and old family," Tanner murmured, his interest picking up.

"Right. Theo sent Sunny to the best schools. She's friends with all the blue bloods of San Francisco. She's known most of these women for years, from before most of them were teenagers. And she knows the gossip surrounding each."

Sean sat back, a look of supreme satisfaction on his face.

"And you think Sunny will gladly jump in to help me find a wife from this illustrious pool?" Tanner asked, knowing that was exactly what his friend had thought.

"I think so," Sean hedged.

"Ah," Tanner said. "There's something more."

The waitress placed their platters before them. Tanner took a moment to savor the pleasing look of the still-sizzling steak. A far cry from what the poor boy from the Tenderloin used to eat.

Those days were gone forever—he didn't even like thinking about them. But he never forgot them. He worked hard to insure he never returned. And he was determined no child of his would ever experience what he'd lived through.

A quick glance around the restaurant assured him he'd succeeded. The men surrounding him were successful businessmen, bankers, financiers, stockbrokers, corporate executives—the movers and shakers of San Francisco. He'd joined their ranks through sheer determination and hard work. He glanced at Sean.

"Let me think about it," he temporized.

Normally he'd give his friend a flat out no. But something made him want to ease his refusal. Maybe it was because years ago Sean had stood by his friend, the rich boy from Woodside and the poor kid from the Tenderloin.

"I'll call Sunny after lunch. I'll give her your number. The two of you can work things out, okay?" Sean asked.

"Sure."

When Sunny called, Tanner would simply mention he had decided to forgo her services. She couldn't be too interested in setting up a girlfriend with a blind date, especially with a man she didn't know.

"Besides your love life, how are things going?" Sean asked, changing the subject.

Soon the two men began to discuss business strategies and successes.

Night had fallen by the time Tanner leaned back in his chair and looked out the big windows that lined one wall of his office. The City by the Bay sparkled. The lights outlining the Bay Bridge seemed to shimmer across the inky water. The Trans America pyramid gleamed in the darkness, lights shining from offices where men and women worked late. He stood and wandered to the window for a closer look. He loved the city. Born and raised here, he never wanted to live anywhere else.

When his phone rang, he wondered who'd call his private line at—he glanced at his watch as he crossed the room—eight thirty-five.

"Wright."

"Hello, is this Tanner Wright?" a breathless feminine voice inquired.

"Speaking."

"Well you're hard to track down. I tried calling you at home several times since six, but there was never an answer. I was sort of surprised you even had a land line. I mean cell service is so good throughout the city. Anyway, I thought you'd be home by six, even with the rush-hour traffic. Now I know why your phone there just rang and rang. You must not have an answering machine. I understand most friends probably call on your cell. Still, it would be nice to have an answering machine. Do you always work so late?"

"Who is this?"

His habits were no one's business but his own.

"Oh, sorry, I guess I jumped ahead. This is Sunny Pritchard. I'm Sean Murphy's cousin. He said you were expecting my call. I tried to call this afternoon, well actually, I wanted to call then, but things kept coming up. And this isn't the kind of thing you want to discuss with a shop full of brides-to-be. So I waited until I thought you'd be home. I've been trying all evening. Finally I wondered if you were still at work and you are. Or I guess you are, I don't hear any restaurant noise in the background. So that's good. I mean that I found you, not that it's good to be working so late."

Tanner wondered when she was going to let up enough so he could get a word in edgewise.

"I wanted to be sure to reach you today if I could so we could get this all cleared up. Sean's my favorite cousin, but he does get carried away sometimes. And some of his schemes are quite outlandish, like this one. I expect you must know that since he said you've been friends from Stanford days. I can't think why we haven't met at some point over the years, but there you are, we haven't. You must not attend his parties. Which shows some sense on your part, they can get pretty wild. Which isn't much like Sean these days, is it? I mean he's become so conservative and all. Probably taking his responsibilities at work seriously. Which will please Uncle Steven."

"Miss Pritchard—"

"Call me Sunny. The thing is, Mr. Wright, I don't run a dating service. Sean said you wanted me to introduce you to some of my friends with an end objective of marriage. I think marriage is a great end objective. One I may have myself some day. But I don't run a dating service. I do weddings. That's usually long after the first date."

"Sean said you ran a bridal salon," Tanner said.

"Yes, I do. Brides and Bows. Actually bows is spelled bo-w-s, but I'm hoping people will think of it as a play on words, *beaux*, like boyfriends, you know? Actually, you should know all about it, your firm gave me the start-up money. Which is why I thought it rather mean to threaten to yank it away. I don't have the money to repay the initial loan yet, but I'm working on it and one day I'll be able to repay you everything. The thing is your Mr. Fielding doesn't seem inclined to take that view. He's trying to force me into liquidation. That would end the business, which seems dumb because then you'd never get all your money back."

"Sean indicated you could use some financial advice."

She was silent for a moment.

"Actually, that's Sean's idea, and probably Aunt Patty's. I'm doing fine if you'd just call off Mr. Fielding. And let's face facts, Mr. Wright, there's no way Tanner Wright of Wright Associates, one of this city's largest and most successful financial services house, is going to bail out a small bridal salon. I'm squeaking out a profit, and I like what I do, but it's not big business. Not like yours is. You can spare the money a little longer."

For some reason her assumption that he wouldn't work with a small firm rankled. He'd started out small himself. One reason he started his venture capital branch was to help others along the way, as well as turn a tidy profit.

Tanner had been fully prepared to refuse her help, but now because she wasn't offering, perversely he wanted it.

"So you won't help me?" he asked softly.

"I think one of San Francisco's most eligible bachelors won't have any trouble attracting women. I've seen your picture in the paper, you know. You're—"

The abrupt silence went on for several seconds until Tanner prompted, "I'm what?"

"Well, let's just say a hunk and let it go at that."

Something touched his sense of humor and he laughed softly. He'd never heard that term referred to himself.

"Maybe you should tell me more."

"I think that would be pointless. I'm glad we had this chat. Don't let Sean railroad you into doing things you don't want."

"I assure you, Ms. Pritchard, I never do anything I don't want." Not anymore.

"Call me Sunny. And I'm glad you are in the position to do just what you want. Sorry to call you at work, but if you keep such long hours you have to expect people will call you there for personal things. Why aren't you home?"

"I beg your pardon?"

"Not my business, I know. But it's getting late. I bet you haven't even had dinner. You should keep better hours," she scolded gently. "I know I work all night sometimes I get so caught up in a design, but I discipline myself to quit and do something frivolous. It restores creative juices, don't you know. And I would think you could use some of that, as well."

"Creative juices?"

Intrigued by this fireball on the phone, Tanner leaned back in his chair and crossed his legs, placing his feet on the edge of the desk.

"I assure you I eat fine, Sunny. But maybe having a wife would insure I kept better hours. Are you sure you won't help in finding me one?" he said smoothly, waiting to hear what she'd say next.

"The problem as I see it, Mr. Wright, besides the fact that

I don't run a dating service, is I know nothing about you. Well, that's not strictly true, because I read the newspapers. But I don't know about your family, your background, what you like to do for fun, what your plans are for the future. How could I match you up with someone if I don't know you? You see the problem? And I do have to work at the shop. If your firm is making threats to foreclose on my note, I have to do something extra to keep going."

"I see."

"Sean's so impulsive. These are my friends we're talking about. I want to make sure they get a good deal, too."

"An introduction is all I believe Sean suggested, not delivering them ready for the altar," Tanner interjected.

"Oh. Well, yes, of course. But even so…I really can't do it."

"I'd be happy to look over your records, perhaps hold off on calling the loan," he said slowly.

At least until he met her. He couldn't remember being so intrigued in years. He found himself curious to meet her in person.

"You're serious, aren't you? You really want me to help you find a bride?"

"No, I want you to introduce me to some eligible women. There's a difference. I can take it from the introduction."

She remained silent a long time.

"What are you looking for?" she asked at last.

"I want someone from a good family with a good pedigree, who knows how to move in society and would be an asset to me in business."

Someone to give him the background he lacked himself. To provide an extended family for his son.

"Sounds like you're looking for a dog or something. Most people come without a pedigree," she muttered.

"Not a dog. A sleek, sophisticated woman who comes from an excellent family."

"You can fall in love to order?" she asked dubiously.

"I don't expect to fall in love. I am sure over time I'll acquire a certain degree of affection for the woman."

"Oh, good grief, now you do sound like you're getting a dog. A degree of affection? What is a degree? Sounds cold-blooded to me. I think you need to do this on your own. I'll tell Sean we talked and decided to let things go the way they were."

"Foreclosure and all?" he asked sharply.

She hesitated. "So that's the way you want it? I cooperate or you yank my business?"

"I believe it's you who hasn't managed to make the loan payments. I would merely be exercising my rights under the terms of the agreement."

Tanner wondered if she cared enough about her business to agree to his terms. He was used to making deals in his favor and he saw nothing to change his methods now.

"I don't know. Wouldn't you consider giving me more time because of your friendship with Sean?"

"No."

"Oh."

The silence stretched out endlessly.

"On the other hand, in exchange for your assistance, I would certainly hold off for a reasonable time. Enough probably to let you recoup and repay the loan," Tanner said, surprising himself.

If the woman didn't want to help, why push the issue?

He'd leave the business end to his employees and go on the way he'd started. This had been Sean's idea, not his.

But he found himself intrigued with Sunny Pritchard, He wanted to meet her. Did she talk as much in person as on the phone? What did she look like? Nothing like his image of a wife, he was certain.

No one who talked this fast and this much could be sleek and sophisticated. Maybe she didn't really know anyone who would measure up to his ideal wife. He had only Sean's word that she knew everyone.

"You're looking for a trophy bride, aren't you? Someone to show off and deck in the family jewels and have other men envy you."

Her tone was sharp.

"Family jewels?" he murmured.

"Everyone has them, gaudy things that some previous generation bought to flaunt their wealth. You don't mention kids, is that part of the deal? Do you want any?"

"Yes, I want a son."

The entire purpose of the exercise was to acquire a son to leave his business and fortune to. He planned to be a better father to his child than he'd ever received. And he wanted his son to have the best mother money could buy.

"To leave everything to, I'm sure. No daughters?"

There was an edge in her voice. He paused for a moment, surprised at the thought.

"Yes, I'd like a daughter or two," he said slowly.

The idea sounded appealing, though he hadn't a clue how to raise a daughter. But his wife would know. She'd be an expert at all that.

"Good, I like little girls better than little boys. Must be from hanging around Sean when we were little. He could really be a pain. I think you can attract the kind of woman you want without any help from me. Go get your picture in the paper again and then start trolling at the parties that abound in the city."

"I'm not sure that'll work," he murmured, knowing she sounded ready to end the conversation. He wanted to extend the call.

"Why not?"

"I took Marie DuPont to the—"

"Marie? No wonder Sean said you needed help. Marie has a drinking problem. Her mother is a drunk and her father gambles all the time. The family had pots of money at one time, but now I hear they are seeking to replenish the family coffers by latching onto some rich young man. Did you ask her out?"

"Yes, I did."

For a moment, he resented the position Marie had placed him in, then shook his head. When he started in the investment arena, he'd had a great deal to learn. Having mastered that, he almost forgot there were other areas in which he was not so knowledgeable. And the ways of San Francisco society were one of them.

Maybe Sean was right, he could use a bit of an insight on the women he considered for a mate.

"So Marie is someone I should stay clear of?"

"If you value your sanity, I would. Besides, if you're looking for someone to help your business, you don't want to be tied to a gambler and a lush."

"I can see your services would be invaluable. I appear to have a lot to learn about this. Will you meet me tomorrow to discuss this further?"

"Your poor-little-me tactics won't work, Mr. Wright. I know how ruthless you can be. You don't need me or anyone else to get you what you want. This is it for me. I'm really not interested. Do your worst about my shop, I'll fight it. Goodbye."

"Goodbye, Sunny," Tanner said to empty air.

Slowly he put the phone down.

Another first—he couldn't remember anyone hanging up on him before.

He looked out the window at the sparkling lights in the other buildings. Sunny Pritchard could be forgiven if she thought she'd had the last word. They hadn't met yet and she didn't know him.

That would change tomorrow. He'd meet her and talk her into helping him. Something told him she was more emotionally involved with her business than most people.

Probably *loved* it.

Sean had been correct, he did need someone who knew her way around society. Sunny might be the exact person to help. And if he decided she was the one, he'd insure she helped, or lose her business.

It would be interesting to see how she handled that. He reached for the phone, dialed a familiar number.

"Sean? It's Tanner. I have a few questions about your cousin Sunny."

2

Tanner pulled his Mercedes into the tight parking space on Union Street. The trendy San Francisco neighborhood had more shops and boutiques per block than any other part of the city. From antique stores to bakeries to fashionable salons, Union Street catered to the elite and rich of San Francisco.

He walked back a block to the discrete gold and white sign: Brides and Bows. He hesitated, unlike him. Usually once he made up his mind he charged ahead, knowing he had weighed all the information before making a decision.

Last night, he'd decided to drop by and meet Sunny in person to further discuss the odd deal Sean proposed. It was past the lunch hour, she should be hard at work, where he hoped to catch her unaware in order to learn a bit more about the intriguing woman.

He held the high cards in this deal, if she didn't cooperate, he'd call the loan and close her business. If it looked like it had potential, he'd put another manager in and see if he could recoup his investment that way.

He pushed open the door, frowning at the tingling bell that sounded. The inside was frilly, lacy and feminine. Gilded French Provincial chairs and a brocade-covered Queen Anne settee formed a small waiting area to the left. A lacy bridal dress was displayed by a mannequin with a sweet young face. Accessories were artistically draped on tables, display cabinets and on the one long counter at the right side of the showroom.

Tanner looked around, feeling decidedly uncomfortable. He felt at home in a boardroom or at a football game—not amid trappings of fairy-tale love and romance.

Tall and muscular, his body was not built for the dainty furniture that welcomed customers. Never one for lace and satin, for a moment he felt totally out of his element. He'd never lived with a woman, nor become more involved than an occasional night in a woman's bed. He knew nothing about bridal wares.

He believed he could go his entire life without knowing.

"Hello, may I help you?"

A tall blonde entered from the doorway in the rear of the store. Elegantly attired in a stylish red suit, her hair worn up in a sophisticated French braid, she looked exactly like what he had in mind for his wife. Had Sean set him up? He knew Tanner wanted someone sleek and sophisticated. Was this Sunny? Had the lure of the foreclosure been Sean's way to force a meeting? Was that why he insisted Tanner use his cousin to find a wife?

"Sunny?" he asked as his eyes skimmed over the discrete curves, the long, slender legs encased in silk stockings. The blonde smiled.

"No, she's in the back working on a dress. I'll get her for you."

Tanner nodded, curiously relieved. He studied the boutique while he waited. He didn't know much about weddings, though he figured he'd find out more than he wanted when he married.

This boutique appeared to have everything a woman could possibly dream up. He looked at frilly little pillows, wondering what they were used for.

"Oh, my goodness, Tanner Wright in the flesh. Come to inspect the merchandise? See what it could get if you put it on the block?"

At the sound of the surprised voice, he turned, and stared right into a pair of dancing blue eyes. He'd never seen merry eyes before, he thought. Slowly he took in the gamine grin, one side a trifle higher than the other. Skin that looked like a soft blushing rose and a wild mop of curly blond hair completed the picture before him. She grinned at him as if in genuine delight.

"You're even better looking in person. Something about black and white newspaper print takes away from the reality, don't you think?"

She came out into the showroom and offered her hand,

"I'm Sunny, as I guess you've figured out. You must be serious about this. I did consider that Sean set me up, but I don't think you're the type to play practical jokes or at least not carry it this far."

"So you're Sunny Pritchard."

He took her hand. Her grip was firm and her skin startling warm and soft. He wanted to hold on to her, to trace that softness with his fingers and see if she felt that soft everywhere. He released her and took a step back, surveying the room to cover his momentary loss of concentration.

"Nice place."

"If you're into this kind of thing, which I suspect you're not."

He looked back at her, studying her from those wild curls down the tailored silk shirt, the woolen pants to—bare feet.

She followed his gaze and grinned.

"I hate shoes. If you were a customer, I'd put them on. That's why I peeped out of the back room first. I always put them on for business. But I really don't like wearing them. Except in winter. Even then I usually wear socks and nothing else unless I go out. Then of course I have to wear something to keep my feet from freezing or looking like some poor street person."

Tanner met her eyes, trying to ignore the image that popped into his mind of Sunny in nothing but wild curls and socks. Awareness shimmered through him and he felt a tightening of desire low down.

"I came to continue our conversation of last night," he said smoothly, refusing to dwell on the tantalizing image that danced in his mind.

"Well, I guess we'll have to since you've gone to all the trouble of coming way over here from Montgomery Street during the height of the day. And I'm grateful you didn't send Mr. Fielding. He's getting to be a bit of a drag. But I don't think we have much to say. What part of no don't you understand?"

"The part that applies to me," he said arrogantly. "Either I get the help I need, or this business becomes mine, lock, stock, and barrel. I'll have a new manager in by tomorrow noon."

He hadn't made it as far as he had by being easy.

She stared up at him, the light in her eyes dimmed. For a moment Tanner wondered if she hadn't really suspected he'd go that far. He didn't have a philanthropic bent regarding business, it was cut and dried. He did whatever he needed to get ahead.

For a moment, he hesitated. And then frowned, disliking the sensation. He who hesitated lost.

So she was pretty. He'd seen beautiful women before, even dated a few. It didn't matter that she was Sean's cousin. This was business pure and simple. She had something he had decided he wanted. And he'd do what it took to get it.

"Well, that's pretty clear."

Sunny put her hands on her hips and stared out of the glass window fronting the street—silent for several long minutes.

Used to silence in negotiating situations, Tanner remained quiet. He'd had years to perfect his skills, he suspected this woman hadn't a clue.

She swung around and glared at him. For an instant he felt a surge of anticipation. So she wasn't going to meekly roll over and play dead?

"First thing I need to do is have my attorney look over the agreement. Probably should have done it when Fielding started nosing around. There's bound to be something I can do to stop you from forcing me to give up my business."

"The contracts we offer are iron-clad. Set up by some of the best attorneys in the city."

"My cousin Clare is pretty good, too," she murmured.

"Another cousin?"

Her eyes narrowed and she stepped closer, tilting back her head to maintain eye contact. Tanner refrained from giving in to the instinct to stand even taller just to see her reaction.

Amusement lurked, she still intrigued him.

"A good attorney," she said.

"So it's war?" he asked.

"If that's your call."

"No, my call is having you introduce me to some eligible single women."

"And if I don't, you take my business. Try to take my business."

"Take this business, no try." His voice brooked no denial. "The choice is yours."

"So let me clarify this. If I introduce you to as many women as I know that fit your requirements for a trophy wife, you'll leave my shop alone?"

She met his gaze, her eyes narrowed.

"At least delay the inevitable," he replied, a sweet flush of triumph sweeping through.

"Wait a minute, no delays. I want some guarantee that I keep the boutique."

"If I get a wife, you get the shop. I'll make it a wedding present."

She frowned.

"That's weird, the groom giving a wedding present to someone beside the bride. But I accept. It'll help tremendously not to have that heavy debt load."

"Don't count your chickens yet, Sunny. I don't have a bride."

"Let me think..."

She walked over to the large picture window and gazed absently out onto busy Union Street, her arms folded beneath her breasts. Turning, Sunny cocked her head as she studied

Tanner. He watched her, amused again by the change in her attitude. Hadn't she suspected he'd play hardball?

Surely her cousin had told her something about him. He wondered what, exactly, Sean had said.

"I can't guarantee a bride, but I can guarantee to introduce you to everyone I think would meet your requirements, once I know what they are. I need to know more about you if I'm to find a compatible match."

Her frown had him wishing she'd smile again.

"Such as?"

"I don't know. I hadn't planned to do it."

She tapped her index finger against her chin.

"Maybe we could get together later at my place and go over some things. I'm really swamped here today and besides, I don't think you'd take to the constant interruptions that are a part of my business. Tonight would work. I need time anyway to think about what I need to know. I've never done anything like this before. I'm not sure what's involved."

"Who's your assistant?" he asked, plunging into the midst of her monologue lest she never stop.

"Eve? She's taken, if you're thinking of her as a possibility. She's been married, and quite happily I might add, for over three years."

Sunny tapped her finger to her chin again and looked him up and down. Walking around him as if surveying a prizefighter, Tanner thought in irritation.

"So you want a trophy wife. Sleek, elegant, sophisticated."

His scowl deepened.

"I think that is a bit harsh a judgment—trophy wife. I want the mother of my children to have an impeccable background."

"You could find her yourself."

"It's faster to have someone screen the candidates for me. This is too important to make a mistake and marry the wrong woman."

"Sounds like business. By all means let's be expeditious," she said, wrinkling her nose.

"A bit different from stocks and bonds, but not much. I'm looking for a long-term merger of two people's lives."

"Oh, my goodness, a merger. Right, that tells me something. Now to find someone who thinks like a computer."

"I don't want a business partner, I want a wife."

"Okay, we'll sit down later and discuss all the sterling attributes you want in a wife and I'll see if any of my friends would fit the bill. And since what you really want is a trophy bride, you'll be happy to learn I know a few women who would be content in that role. They like money, like spending it on clothes and jewelry to adorn themselves, don't want to waste energy on emotions like love. They'd do you proud."

"Sunny, phone, it's Joanne Pembroke," Eve called from the archway.

"Oh, right. Excuse me, I need to take this call, business you know."

"Take it, I'll wait."

She looked as if she wanted to tell him no, but she turned and hurried back through the doorway.

Eve stayed with Tanner, smiling slowly.

"She's a whirlwind, isn't she? I can't keep up with her, so I no longer try."

"I'd have expected her to dress a bit more—"

He hesitated, not wanting to insult Eve's boss to her employee. But he knew clothes made a difference in business. It had been one of the first things he'd discovered. People are influenced by what other people wear. An expensive suit with all the right accessories gave the impression of confidence, assurance, and wealth. He'd used that technique when he first started. It'd made the difference in more than one business deal.

"You've been with Sunny for a couple of years?" Tanner asked.

"Ever since she started the boutique. I was looking for something to fill my days. She more than provided that." Eve smiled again.

Tanner thought she was probably a major asset to Sunny's boutique.

"Business doing well?" he asked.

Her smile faded.

"You have to discuss that with Sunny. That's not my place."

"Probably not doing so or you would have given me a resounding yes."

He walked over to one of the wedding dresses.

"How much?" he asked.

"That one's twelve hundred dollars."

"For a single dress? Worn one afternoon?"

He shook his head in disbelief. That money could be invested and start earning a return, instead of being frittered away for an hour's ceremony.

"Why is it on display?" He glanced around. "There aren't any others."

"We made it up for a woman who changed her mind and eloped. We're hoping someone will see it and want to buy it."

"Did she pay for the dress?"

"Only the down payment. We took a loss on it. Sunny's hoping that by displaying it, someone will walk in the door, see it, and fall in love with it."

Love.

That was what Sunny dealt in.

Tanner felt uncomfortable. He didn't believe in the emotion and hoped that wasn't going to prove a stumbling block in working with Sunny. Obviously she was a hopeless romantic, even based her business on the nebulous emotion of love.

"Sorry about that," Sunny said as she hurried back into the showroom. "I've been waiting to talk with her for ages. She's been out of town. Her wedding is only three weeks away. I wondered if she'd get back in time for it. Now, what else do we need to do? I have a ton of work waiting."

Sunny smiled at Eve and stopped some distance from Tanner. He wondered why the distance. For a moment he had the urge to walk right up to her, crowd her against that counter and—

She wasn't very tall, the top of her head barely cleared his shoulder. Her lips looked soft and gentle, damp when she licked them. Her eyes were her best feature, and she frankly watched him, a hint of wariness in her gaze. He wanted to see the shining light that had sparkled when he'd first met her.

"I thought I'd go over your books, see where you stand, to give me a better feeling for what's needed here, or how far behind you truly are."

She swallowed. "My books," she repeated, looking at Eve as if for help.

Eve smiled and shrugged her shoulders. "Don't look at me. I don't keep the books."

"Yes, well, actually this is not a very good time," Sunny said, obviously stalling.

"And when would be good?"

He suspected instantly that her books must be a total disaster. He wasn't an accountant, he was a financial advisor. His clients were multi-million-dollar corporations with up-to-the-minute record-keeping software.

"Tonight, maybe. You're coming over, right?"

He nodded.

"Eight be all right?"

"Yes."

She gave him her address and walked with him to the door. He'd never been escorted from anyplace, but that was the feeling he got from Sunny. She was kicking him out, nicely, but definitely.

"Dress casually, I will," she said as she opened the door and almost pushed him out.

Tanner heard the bell jingle and the door click behind him. He glanced up the street, wondering whether to confront the woman now or give in to the amusement that simmered. It had been a long time since he'd felt like this.

If ever.

His watch read precisely eight o'clock when Tanner knocked at the door to Sunny's Chestnut Street apartment. The building smelled musty and old, while parking on the street had proved to be an abomination.

When she opened the door, he felt a clutch of feeling as she smiled up at him.

"You're prompt, but then I expected that. Have you been waiting out in the hall for the exact moment to knock? Most people arrive a few minutes early or late, but I could have set my clock by you."

"No need to wait, I timed my arrival to the minute."

She looked at his suit.

"I thought I said casual."

"I came from work. And since this is business, I thought this appropriate."

She had changed into a vibrant pink and blue warm-up suit and pulled her hair away from her face in clips. Her feet were bare.

"Your loss. I like comfort myself. Come in and sit. Can I get you something to drink? Or eat? Did you have dinner?"

"You're not my mother, Sunny. I don't want nor need anything. Let's get to the business at hand."

Tanner refused to be sidetracked by her hospitality or by his own fascination with her toes.

"All men want to do is cut to the chase, never mind the niceties of social living. I don't know why women bother. Yet we seem to generation after generation."

Tanner ignored her complaint as he walked into her living room. It suited her. Large comfortable chairs and a plump sofa were arranged to provide a warm welcome. He sank into one of the chairs and almost smiled. It provided the perfect support for his large frame. He wondered if she'd bought it for male friends. The smile faded as the thought disturbed him.

Did Sunny have a lot of male friends? Close enough to drop by from time to time?

"Good grief, we haven't even started and you're frowning already. What's wrong?"

"Nothing. Let's begin. I have an early appointment tomorrow."

"And so don't want to stay out late. All right."

She sat on the sofa, tucked her feet up beneath her and drew a yellow pad and pencil from the coffee table.

"Yellow's good for creativity, did you know that?" she murmured as she wrote his name on the top.

"I didn't. Are we getting creative with my requirements?"

"Nope. I just like yellow. How old are you?"

"What does that have to do with anything?" he asked.

She looked up.

"Well, while some people might not mind being a trophy wife of an older man with pots of money, some would. So I have to know how old you are—"

"I'm hardly an older man. I'm thirty-five," he snapped, already feeling exasperated with Sunny and with himself for allowing this to proceed.

"I'm twenty-six myself. Most of the friends I have who are still eligible for the marriage stakes are around my age. Some might not want to date an older man."

"For heaven's sake, I'm not an older man. Thirty-five is a man's prime."

"Right—and exactly what I expected a man of thirty-five to say," she muttered, throwing him a look. "What's your favorite color?"

Tanner glared at her. "Sunny," he said, clamping down on

the anger that began to simmer. "I don't have a favorite color and what the hell would it matter in being introduced to some woman?"

She sighed and looked at him, her expression serious.

"Tanner, I need to get a feel for who you are and what you like so I can talk about you to friends. I can't do this if you are going to question every question I ask. If you like green, you're probably a genius. More geniuses like the color green than any other color. If blue—"

"Black. If I have to like a color, make it black," he bit out.

"Matches your heart, eh?"

She jotted a note on her pad.

"What's your favorite color?" he asked before she finished writing.

"Mine? Pink. Why?"

He held her gaze for a long moment. Then shrugged.

"Just curious."

He rose and took off his suit jacket, placing it across the arm of the other chair. Loosening his tie, he sat back down, sprawled his long legs out before him, hooked his thumbs beneath his belt and stared at her.

"Relaxed, huh?" She grinned.

He nodded, his gaze direct. Sunny caught her breath, looking down at her pad as if flustered.

"Something wrong," he asked as something eased inside.

Maybe he wasn't the only one to feel this unexpected pull of attraction, of strong awareness. She was a pretty woman, soft and feminine. Being around her made him more conscious of being a man. It wasn't just that he hadn't had a woman in a while, there was more.

Something about her claimed his interest. Yet she met none of the requirements in what he wanted in a wife. There was nothing sleek or elegant about her. She appeared bright, funny and a bit irreverent. He thought of sunshine and flower gardens when around her. Did other men?

Again the thought disturbed. Why should he care what other men thought about Sunny? He was using her to gain his own goal—the perfect blue-blood wife, with strong ties to an old San Francisco family. He'd firm up his own place in society and provide the best background possible for any children.

She shook her head, her eyes firmly on her pad.

"Nothing's wrong. What's your favorite food?"

"Tacos."

"Tacos?"

She looked up, startled.

"Something wrong with tacos?"

"No, only I thought you'd like caviar or filet mignon or something ritzy."

"I like tacos. What's your favorite?"

"Shrimp, boiled, shelled, cooled and with lots of cocktail sauce."

"I would have pictured you with chocolate," he said.

She flashed that gamine grin he started to expect around her.

"I do like chocolate—dark chocolate. It'd be perfect after the shrimp."

For the next two hours Sunny asked questions, what books did he read, which movies he liked, which ones he didn't. She asked where he'd traveled and vacationed. What

FINDING A WIFE FOR TANNER | 39

his favorite thing was to do on a lazy Saturday. For every question she asked him, he asked one of her in return. When she asked him about growing up, he'd turned the subject.

Finally she asked him outright about his parents.

"They're both dead," Tanner said flatly.

"How awful, I'm so sorry."

Her blue eyes held sadness, concern.

"It happened a long time ago," he said shortly.

He didn't need her sympathy.

"We can skip that for now. It's who you are today that will entice a woman."

Tanner tried to find out what made Sunny tick as the evening wore on. She perplexed him. She didn't fit any mold he knew. He wanted an explanation.

According to Sean, she turned her back on the wealth her stepfather offered, and plunged instead into earning her own living. The schooling she'd gratefully accepted, but nothing beyond.

Tanner was not used to being around women. The few he knew seemed to expect others to wait on them, to provide them with enough money to purchase everything they wanted and give them the lifestyle they sought—using his money.

It was what he expected of his wife. She'd know how to buy furnishings for his home to impress people. She'd be able to dress appropriately for his position in the business community. And maybe he'd purchase those jewels Sunny had spoken about.

Only nothing gaudy, something tasteful and expensive—only the best for his wife. There was nothing wrong in a man making sure others knew he had attained financial security by the baubles he bought his wife.

"That's enough for one night," Sunny said, tossing her scribbled notes on the table and stretching.

The top of the running suit came a bit above her waist, exposing a strip of pale skin. Tanner's gaze instantly dropped there and he wondered if that skin felt softer than her hand had been. He'd like to explore that stretch of skin and find out.

Heck, he'd like to explore a whole lot more than just that small sliver of skin. He'd like to explore Sunny Pritchard herself from tousled curls to pink toes.

"Did you bring your financial records home?" he asked.

She'd filled the time with questions, but made no mention of the second part of the deal. Biting her lip, she looked at him, indecision clearly written on her face.

"Actually, I did. But you don't have to look at them tonight. Another time maybe?" she asked brightly. "It is getting late. If I know you, you'll want to be in the office early tomorrow for that appointment. Right?"

"Tonight's fine."

He ignored her red herring.

"I thought you had an early appointment in the morning."

He smiled.

"Get the books, Sunny."

"You look like a wolf who's ready to pounce."

"Wolves don't pounce, kittens pounce. Wolves stalk, waiting for the right moment to spring on their prey and take them down."

Her eyes widened and she stared at him for a long moment.

Sighing long and hard when Tanner remained silent, Sunny rose and flounced into the hallway, resentment evident in every step. Returning moments later, she carried a satchel of papers and one binder. Reluctantly, she crossed the room and thrust them out to him. She almost dragged her feet like a kid, he thought as he looked at the satchel. He shouldn't have been surprised. He knew small businesses often did their record-keeping differently from major corporations, but this handbag of papers was worse than he expected.

"Do you have any clue how you're doing?" he asked in shock.

"Pretty good, I think. Well, maybe not all that well. I have trouble making ends meet sometimes. Other times I have some extra cash. That's why Sean thought you should check these things out. An even cash flow would go a long way in helping to make the business a success, don't you think?"

"Undoubtedly. I'll look at this and get back to you."

He rose and donned his jacket. Actually he planned to have his accountant make some sense out of the mess. He wasn't going to waste his time.

And once Stuart straightened out the records, he'd have him teach some basic accounting to Sunny Pritchard. If she was serious about running a business, she needed better skills than this.

"What are you doing for lunch on Friday?" she asked.

For a moment he wondered if she were asking him out. "Why?"

She was Sean's cousin, a woman who was helping him find a wife. She wouldn't invite him on a date. He wasn't sure she even liked him.

"I think Carmella Randolph would be a good candidate. I've been thinking about her as we talked. I'll invite her to lunch on Friday. You can accidentally happen upon us. Then I'll invite you to join us. You and Carmella can take it from there," she said, her eyes going forlornly to her papers.

"What time Friday and where?"

"Carmella loves that restaurant near Battery and Montgomery. Sabrina's. How about twelve-thirty?"

"You're on. See you then."

He picked up his jacket and the satchel and headed for the door. Sunny followed him. He could smell her perfume, the fragrance familiar. He had it—strawberry. Fresh and wholesome like she was.

He stopped by the door. Sunny stopped beside him and looked up. Without thinking, without giving any analysis, he leaned over and brushed his lips across hers. She felt as soft as he'd thought she'd be. And six times sweeter.

"Good night."

He left quickly, before she could say a word. And for once he felt the honors were his. She'd been stunned, too much to even think of talking. But the joke was on him, he thought a few minutes later as he climbed into his car. He could still feel that petal softness, that sweetness about her. Something intrigued him about Sunny Pritchard. He'd best remember theirs was a business deal and ignore the rest.

And avoid kissing her in the future.

By ten the next morning, Tanner gave up. He tossed his gold pen down and shoved the prospectus away. He'd been trying to concentrate on the new proposal since his early appointment had ended, but his curiosity ran rampant. He couldn't concentrate. He wanted answers on Sunny's situation.

He quickly went down the hall to Stuart's office. The man had papers piled around, in some sort of order, but it looked like mildly controlled chaos to Tanner.

"Get anywhere on Brides and Bows?" he asked.

Stuart looked up and grimaced.

"This is the biggest mess I've ever seen. Apparently she jots things down on scrap paper, then drops everything into an envelope until it gets too crowded, then she starts up another envelope. Some bills have notes on them that they've been paid, others don't, yet she doesn't carry the balance on the next one so they have to have been paid. She didn't include the checkbook."

"Will you be able to get a financial reading?" Tanner asked.

"I can get something. How accurate, I can't guarantee. This woman needs a few basic accounting lessons."

"Let me know when you're finished. I'll get the checkbook somehow."

At five Stuart returned the satchel and binder to Tanner, totally exasperated. He'd done as much as he could, but had pages of notes and questions. Tanner thanked him for the effort and glanced at his watch. It was too late to call her at work. What he'd really like to do was take these books over to her house and sit her down and demand she go through everything with him. And answer every one of Stuart's questions.

But it'd take more than a couple of hours. Maybe she'd have time that weekend. Not Saturday. He couldn't make Saturday, he had promised the director he'd be in this Saturday for sure.

Maybe Sunday. He'd have to check with her. Later, once she was home.

Tanner first called at seven. There was no answer. Impatient with the delay, he slammed down the receiver. Acting on a hunch, he called her shop. The phone rang and rang. Not there. He tried her home again at seven-thirty, then at eight, then nine.

He should have gotten her cell number. She obviously wasn't home.

"Hello?"

"Sunny? This is Tanner."

"Hi, what's up?"

"Where have you been?"

"Me? Out. What do you want? Why are you calling me at home?"

"We went over your books today. You almost drove my accountant into quitting."

He settled back in his chair, waiting to hear what she had to say. He didn't want to admit how much he'd looked forward to hearing her voice again.

"Well, I have been meaning to get everything organized, but I'm so busy with other things I haven't had the time. I'm much more interested in sewing dresses and matching the precisely right accessories than spending hours doing boring bookkeeping. And Eve doesn't do books. Not that she should, it is my business. Um, did he say how things look?"

"It's hard to determine without your current checkbook. You didn't give me that."

"Well of course not. That's my money, I'm not just handing it over to someone because they want to study my records. I need that, I pay bills, pay Eve, I can't just hand that over. I can read you the balance if you have to have it, but I'm not giving it up."

"We need to see the individual entries, run a reconciliation. If you have any extra cash, we should explore investment opportunities."

"What? Like there would be more than one? Okay, I want to invest any extra money in something that will pay big dividends that I can use next month if I'm short."

"Everybody wants that."

"Well, isn't that what you do? I mean, everything I've heard about you indicates you're some sort of wunderkind about investments. Making millions for companies who call you in to turn their economics around. Have you ever lost a dime?"

"Yes, I've lost a dime, but made a dollar as a result. I've done all right."

"Is that some macho male kind of deprecation? I thought men liked to boast of their prowess."

The only prowess he'd like to boast about right now was sexual. The thought stunned him. He didn't think of Sunny in a sexual manner. She was helping him find a wife. She was the go-between, not a candidate. She didn't fit his ideal wife at all.

She wasn't particularly tall. Her hair would never be

considered sleek, and sophistication was just a word to her. She probably slipped off her shoes in church.

Yet he couldn't forget how soft and warm her skin felt. Couldn't forget the merry dancing lights in her blue eyes. Maybe calling her hadn't been such a good idea, after all, he thought, shifting in his chair.

"Tanner?"

"I'm still here."

"When did you want to get together? Let's not discuss this while we have lunch with Carmella. She's got tons of money and would love to invest it under your direction. But I think you ought to wait before suggesting investments to her until you marry her, if she's the one. I want my business situation kept confidential."

"I never mix clients' portfolios," he said stiffly, a bit uncertain whether this Carmella was going to be the right one. Something about the name, he thought.

"Well, that's fine, then. What did you do today, besides make tons of money? Did you quit work early? Tanner—are you still at your office?"

"Yes,."

"That's terrible. Do you realize it's after nine at night? I'm getting ready for bed and left work hours ago. I can't believe you're still there. For one thing, you'll ruin your eyes with all that reading. And for another, how do you get dinner? Or do you eat around midnight. That's not good for you to eat and then go to bed."

"I might have left earlier if you'd been home. I've been trying to reach you since seven."

"Oh. Well, I was out."

He remained silent, wondering who she'd been out with, where they'd gone, what they'd done.

"It wasn't a real date or anything, just dinner with a friend. Actually he wanted it to be a date, but I didn't. I just wanted to catch up on news and see him. But you know how men can be. Of course you do, you are one."

"Did he try something?"

A dark anger took told.

"No, of course not. He wanted to go out dancing after we ate. I'm wearing slacks, what kind of dork would I look going dancing with a guy while I'm in slacks. I mean people might have trouble telling which was which."

"I doubt that, unless his hair is longer than yours," Tanner murmured, wondering who the man had been.

Sunny laughed. The sound was light and full, and reminded Tanner of her eyes, how lights seemed to sparkle from the blue depths. He could imagine them half closed as she laughed, wearing that trifle lopsided smile.

"Cute, Tanner. I didn't realize you had a sense of humor. I always think of you as some macho stud. Ruthless, swashbuckling your way through the financial district like a pirate of old. You'd have made it big on the Barbary Coast and thrown fear into all the gamblers."

"You've thought about me?" he murmured. "Since when?"

"I saw your pictures in the paper a while back. But I don't want to talk about that. How about Saturday?"

"For what?"

"To get together to talk about my books. I'll be glad to tell people that I work with Tanner Wright, he handles my business accounts. Think how I can impress—"

"Saturday's out," he interrupted.

"Oh? Why?"

"I can't make Saturday. How about Sunday?"

"Sure. No. Wait a minute. Sunday I have a barbecue to attend at my aunt's house. Come with me. I can bring a date. You wouldn't be a date, but you could come with me and we could talk on the way. It's Sean's mother, my aunt Patty, maybe you know her already?"

"Yes, I do."

It'd been several years since he'd seen Sean's parents, but they'd always welcomed him in their home.

"Then you'll fit right in. Only this is casual. Do not wear a suit."

"I know how to dress."

"Well you couldn't prove it by me. This will be a casual afternoon, one for relaxing and enjoying yourself. And eating. Aunt Patty fixes the best food in the world. She's a much better cook than my mother or grandmother. I wonder where she learned to do that? I don't cook much myself, do you?"

"Just the minimum to get by. What time Sunday?"

"Your car is probably fancier than mine. Can you drive?"

Tanner hesitated, then smiled. He enjoyed driving his Mercedes, but he also had something else for Miss Thinks-She-Knows-It-All.

"Yes, I'll drive. What time shall I pick you up?"

"About ten. That will get us down there early enough to help set up. We can talk on the way down. It's about an hour's drive."

"I know where Woodside is," he said patiently.

She laughed again.

"Of course you do. But if things really go well with Carmella and you two make other plans for Sunday, we can meet some other time. I won't mind. And I won't tell anyone you're coming, that way if you don't, no one will think you bagged out at the last minute."

He'd almost forgotten the planned meeting at Friday's lunch. But no matter how much he felt Carmella might fit his requirements, he wouldn't pass up on Sunday with Sunny. He wanted to hear her explanations about her books. And to see her sparkling eyes again.

"I won't make other plans," he said firmly.

3

Tanner paused in the entryway to the restaurant. He kept his expression neutral, but grimaced inside. The place looked like a restaurant women liked. He'd asked Rachel about it before leaving his office and she told him it specialized in pasta dishes and salads.

With the flowers and plants hanging around, he felt like he was walking into a blasted garden. He didn't need all the latticework and white wrought-iron furniture, but supposed it appealed to something in the female psyche.

Scanning the large floor area, he noted at least a half dozen men, but the majority of the customers were women. He spotted Sunny in the far corner. Weaving his way through the tables, he kept her in sight as he moved to join her.

She still reminded him of sunshine. She'd subdued her hair somewhat today, tying it back in some sort of arrangement. Soft golden tendrils framed her face and his fingers itched to brush them away. Did it feel as silky as it looked? If he brushed it back, would the curls entwine themselves around his fingers, as if they didn't want to let go?

He couldn't help risking a peek at her feet. Shod today. The long, dark slacks tapered around graceful ankles, and the silk blouse was a light pink, which enhanced her coloring.

He glanced at the woman seated beside her. Flashy

popped instantly into mind. She wore her hair short, better to display the sparkling diamonds swinging from her ears, he thought cynically. The diamond tennis bracelet that encircled her wrist glittered as she waved her hand around in emphasis.

When he reached their table, Sunny looked up.

"Why, Tanner, what an unexpected surprise. How are you? What are you doing here?"

"Hello, Sunny."

He wanted to tell her to cool the surprise and enthusiasm a bit before Miss Diamonds caught on that this wasn't a spontaneous meeting.

"I planned to meet a friend for lunch, but I appear to have been stood up. I saw you across the room, so thought I'd stop by and say hello," Tanner said easily.

Subterfuge obviously came more readily to him than to Sunny.

"Would you like to join us?" She turned to the sleek woman beside her, "You don't mind do you, Carmella?"

"Not at all." Carmella smiled warmly at Tanner, her eyes taking in his expensive suit.

Sunny quickly made introductions and signaled the waitress that they needed another menu. Once the meals had been ordered, she beamed at her two companions

"This is great, Tanner. I haven't seen you in ages. Carmella, you know Tanner is a good friend of my cousin Sean's."

"I didn't know that, but I feel as if I already know you, Tanner. I've seen your picture in the paper on numerous occasions. Always in the business section, I might add," Carmella said, her eyes almost hungry as they studied him.

"Tanner works very hard, that's why he's such a success," Sunny said.

Carmella looked amused as she exchanged glances with Tanner.

"I assure you, Sunny, I know how successful Tanner Wright is."

Tanner leaned back and studied the woman Sunny had introduced him to. On the surface she appeared to be exactly what he ordered. She made small talk easily, yet wasn't afraid to show her interest.

As the meal progressed, however, Tanner became irritated to notice he didn't care one way or another about Carmella Randolph and her opinions.

"Do you enjoy the opera, Tanner?" she asked as she ate daintily, pushing the salad around on the plate rather than take a healthy bite.

Sunny looked up. He noticed she'd been eating like she hadn't had food in a month. First a salad, then a large plate of linguine. The sourdough bread disappeared at an alarming rate. Yet she remained as slender as a reed. How did she do it?

"I'm sorry, Carmella, you asked about the opera?" Tanner said when Sunny frowned at him and nodded her head toward Carmella as if prompting him.

"I asked if you liked opera?"

"No."

Sunny raised her eyebrows.

"That's it, Tanner, just no? Why not? I think some of the best operas have been performed by the San Francisco Opera Company. *La Boheme* was a wonderful rendition last season."

"I don't care for opera," he said.

"Oh."

She looked blankly at Carmella.

"Any of the arts?" she asked.

"The symphony is fine. I enjoy good music, but not people singing in a language I don't understand."

"My parents have season tickets to the symphony, perhaps you'd care to join us some evening," Carmella said, her smile polished, her eyes displaying interest.

Tanner smiled. "Perhaps. I, too, have season tickets."

"Imagine that, you two have probably attended the same symphony performances and didn't even know each other. Now you do," Sunny said brightly.

Her smiled looked a trifle desperate, Tanner thought cynically. Was she concerned about something?

"Carmella is a big 49er's fan, aren't you, Carmella?" Sunny said when the silence had stretched out several seconds.

The woman shrugged.

"I used to be when we were in school. I think I've outgrown that fascination with football now. Though men never seem to, do they, Tanner?" she said archly.

He shook his head. "Apparently not. I'm still an avid fan."

"Season tickets, I assume," she inquired.

"Of course."

"Isn't that nice?" Sunny said. "Maybe you can make up a group and we can all go see a game."

"Perhaps."

Tanner knew his holding back was annoying Sunny. But he refused to commit himself to Carmella Randolph.

On the surface she seemed to meet most of his requirements, but there was something about her that did not quite gel with what he sought for the mother of his son. Three times she'd mentioned her father's money. He might not mind giving unlimited carte blanche to his wife but he didn't want her bragging about it.

When he'd finished eating, Tanner caught Sunny's eye.

"Glad I ran into you today, Sunny. Thanks for inviting me to join you both for lunch. Carmella, it's been a pleasure."

He rose and leaned over Sunny, deliberately dropping his head until he could feel her breath on his cheek. If the scene looked intimate, so much the better. He wanted to make sure Carmella had no illusions about any follow-up calls from him.

"I'll pick you up at ten on Sunday, be ready," he said loudly enough for Carmella to hear.

With another polite smile at Carmella, he straightened and left. The startled look on Sunny's face had been priceless.

Smiling as he walked back to his office, he wondered how long it would be before he heard from her. He was sure there'd be a lecture in this for him.

Sunny had surprised him at lunch with her reticence. Obviously she knew how to be quiet when the occasion called for it. But if she'd hoped to have Carmella outshine her, she'd mistaken the situation.

For a moment he wondered if she'd deliberately brought the most inappropriate woman she knew to lunch. But that didn't seem like Sunny—she was too forthright. She probably thought Carmella fit.

And on the surface, at first, he'd thought so, as well. But a few minutes in her company sufficed to show the error in that. She'd bored him.

As he waited for the elevator, he was startled to realize

he'd probably never grow bored with Sunny. Of course he was beginning to know her and like her. Much as he liked Sean. Maybe knowing she was his cousin made the difference.

Knowing she was not at all what he wanted in a wife, he could relax around her. There were no hidden agendas. She'd help him out, in exchange, he'd hold off closing down her business.

"Tanner, you have an irate caller on line one, but she refuses to give her name," Rachael announced mid afternoon.

He smiled in anticipation. He knew he could count on Sunny. Even after such a brief acquaintance, he knew enough about her to predict her reactions to certain situations.

"Thanks, Rachel."

He pressed the appropriate button.

"Hello, Sunny," he said.

"How did you know it was me, I didn't tell your secretary who I was. I didn't want to give rise to gossip, but I should have walked over there and beat some sense into that thick head of yours. Carmella is definitely interested. Aren't men supposed to know the signs? I expected you to ask for her phone number at the very least, although I can give it to you if you like. On my way back to work I realized that asking her out while I was sitting there might have been a tad awkward, but honestly, Tanner, saying you were picking me up on Sunday made it sound to Carmella like there is something between us. She asked if she'd be poaching—"

"Sunny, take a breath and let me get a word in edgewise," he ordered.

There was silence on the line. A fuming silence, to be sure.

"I didn't ask for her number because I have no intention

in asking her out. And if she thinks we have something going, all the better, she won't pester me," he said ruthlessly.

"Pester? I thought you'd like her. She's sophisticated, pretty, elegant. Her family is old, old San Francisco and has tons of money. She went to all the best schools. Carmella doesn't have to work, her father settled a huge trust on her. She wears clothes to die for, and has scads of friends. Gets invited to all the in parties and social events. Gives half of them. What more do you want?"

"For one thing, I don't want someone constantly bragging about her father's wealth. I didn't know whether I was supposed to match him dollar for dollar, tell her I could buy and sell him tomorrow or be impressed."

"Oh."

"And I didn't like the way she cut you out of the conversation. I want someone a bit more gracious."

"Gracious. Good grief. All right. Maybe Carmella is a bit too much. She and I aren't really friends, just acquaintances. Prior to lunch today I hadn't seen her in ages. When you talk to people at parties, you don't have to spend much time with them. But she beats Marie."

"We agree on that."

"I can't ask anyone else to lunch until sometime next week," she said.

"I'm a patient man."

"Right, I can feel that patience oozing out of you. That must explain why you are such a success, you *patiently* wait for things to happen. You never grab someone by the throat and shake them up, do you?"

Her voice dripped with sarcasm.

"I might grab you by the throat next time I see you, especially if the next candidate is as unsuitable as Carmella. What are you doing tonight?" he asked.

"I've got a date."

"With whom?"

Tanner didn't stop to analyze the surge of emotion that coursed through him.

He gripped the receiver tightly, a scowl on his face. Who was she going out with? Someone she'd known a long time, or a new man?

"You said you didn't need a mother, well I don't need a big brother. You don't have the right to question my dates. I've agreed to help you out, but that's all. Our two lives are separate. Besides, you wouldn't know him even if I told you his name. He doesn't run in the same circles as you."

"Tell me his name. It's a simple question, simply curiosity."

Tanner heard the edge in his voice, but he didn't care. He wanted to know who she planned to see tonight.

"Ha. If the phone company didn't use such strong cable, the heat across this line would have melted the connection."

He clamped down on his furious retort and took a calming breath.

"I merely asked whom you were going out with."

"Joseph Thurmond Sanger the Fourth. Does that make you happy?" she said in a rush, anger coloring her tone.

"And who is he to you?"

"A good friend. A very good friend. Maybe one of the best friends I've got. And maybe after tonight he'll be an even better friend. An intimate friend, if you know what I mean.

Not that it is any of your business, Tanner Wright. I'm trying to get you a date, you don't have to worry about me finding dates. I have more than I can manage. I've got to go. See you Sunday."

The connection was severed before he could reply. With suspect calmness he replaced the receiver. Someone needed to teach her to stop hanging up on him.

Standing, Tanner prowled to the window, his dark thoughts focused on Joseph Thurmond Sanger the Fourth. How long would it take to find out who the man was and what his relationship to Sunny was?

His true relationship, not the lover she'd implied.

Sunday Tanner donned well-worn jeans and comfortable black motorcycle boots. His shirt was Western in style, and a bit faded from dozens of washings. Because the day looked warm, he left the top two buttons unfastened. Rolling up his sleeves until his forearms were unencumbered, he stood before the mirror. Gone was the sleek businessman he normally saw. In his place was an image of the poor boy from the Tenderloin. Jeans were ubiquitous across class lines, yet he remembered when that was all he had to wear, torn and faded as they'd been.

Today he'd be right in style. He'd seen a lot of teenagers wearing ripped jeans, but he couldn't find it stylish. It brought back vivid, painful memories of the grinding poverty from his childhood.

But no matter what his feelings, he knew how to blend in. Today was casual, he'd go casual. He was comfortable in this attire, even if it reminded him of the past. He checked his gold watch and noted the time.

He'd arrive at Sunny's a few minutes early, go up and wait for her in that frilly apartment. And find out about her date on Friday.

He'd thought of little else yesterday when he should have been thinking more about the boys he'd been with at the Big Brothers event. Going through the motions of pickup basketball games, or shooting pool with the older boys, his thoughts had centered around Sunny all day.

He already had an image of Joseph Thurmond Sanger the Fourth. Tall, thin, but athletic. The only son of old family money. Attended the best schools and without raising a finger could command the adoration of impressionable young women.

Scowling at his thoughts, Tanner turned to head for Sunny's. Standing before her apartment door twenty minutes later, he wondered how long she'd keep him waiting as he rang the doorbell. Somehow she hadn't struck him as the epitome of punctuality. Sunny swung the door wide.

"Hi, Tanner, you're early."

She leaned against the door for a moment and let her eyes wander down his body. The tingling awareness he felt around her sprang to life, as did a certain part of his anatomy that he wished would not

"No traffic."

He crossed inside before she noticed anything.

"Come in," she said a bit testily to his back.

The door closed with a decided slam.

Tanner turned and studied her, from her springy curls to

the snug pullover T-shirt that outlined that slender body like a second skin. He wanted to lick his lips when he dropped his gaze to her hips. The jeans she wore were taut over rounded flesh and he itched to touch the denim to see how tight those jeans were stretched.

He looked up into her eyes and felt that same lightness he'd experienced the first time around her. Her eyes danced with humor and happiness. Her smile warmed him and welcomed.

"I'll just be a minute."

Was her voice softer than usual? He couldn't tell, only knew it sounded hesitant. If she were truly angry about his pushing in, she'd have said something.

One thing about a sassy woman, you always knew where you stood.

"You are going to wear shoes, aren't you?" he asked as his eyes followed her down the hall, her bare feet making no sound on the carpet. "

Of course. I'm almost ready. Have a seat."

She disappeared and Tanner wandered around her small living room, looking at the pictures on the walls, shaking his head again at the blatant romanticism of the woman. She was in for a rude awakening some day, he thought. Better to contract a kind of business marriage like he planned and forget all the hearts and flowers stuff.

"Ready."

Smiling gaily, Sunny rejoined Tanner.

She carried a small purse with a long strap, which she slung over her head and across one shoulder. The strap nestled between her breasts. Tennis shoes clad her feet. When he looked at them, she laughed softly.

"I'll take them off at Aunt Patty's but I'll wear them until I get there."

Leaving the apartment, Tanner waited while she locked her door, then headed for the parking space he'd found in front. He stopped by his shiny black Harley-Davidson.

Sunny looked at the motorcycle then looked at Tanner. He smiled slowly at the puzzled expression in her eyes. Catching her off guard buoyed his spirits.

"Never underestimate the opposition."

"Wow, I never thought you'd own a motorcycle. I almost expected a limo."

"I thought it too pretty a day to waste in a car," he said easily, relishing the knowledge that he'd thrown her off base.

Unfastening the two helmets, he handed her one.

She drew it on, her eyes big as saucers.

"Well, you are full of surprises, aren't you? I never expected this. Not in a hundred years. If not a limo, I thought your tastes would run to a Porsche or a Lamborghini or something outrageously fancy and expensive. But this, wow! Do you know how to drive it?"

"This is outrageously fancy and expensive--for a bike. And of course I know how to drive it. Didn't anyone ever warn you against stereotyping people?"

Sunny shrugged and snapped the chin strap.

"Ever ridden one of these before?" he asked as he snapped his own strap.

She shook her head, eyeing the machine with scarcely concealed excitement.

"You'll like it."

The way she threw herself into things, she'd probably end up offering to buy it by the end of the day.

He straddled the big machine, and patted the seat behind him. "Climb on."

She swung her leg over and sat gingerly in the deep leather seat.

"Scoot forward and hold on to me," he instructed as he turned the key.

The powerful machine roared to life as Sunny pressed herself against him, gripping around his waist with hands that trembled slightly.

"You're not worried, are you?"

He felt her shake her head against him.

"I've been riding bikes since I was a kid. This was the only transportation I could afford for a long time. We'll be perfectly safe," he promised.

She relaxed her grasp a fraction. If he'd had any idea the torment riding double with Sunny would put him through, he'd have ordered a limo for today and sat as far from her as possible.

Her scent swirled around them, strawberries and woman. He knew once they started the breeze would waft the scent away, but as he moved slowly out into traffic, it filled his senses.

Her thighs pressed against his, her arms hugged him around his waist, and her firm breasts flattened against the muscles of his back. For a moment he wondered what she'd do if he turned around, draped her thighs over his and pressed those delectable breasts to his chest.

Blast it all, he had to change this line of thought before

something happened that he'd regret.

She was Sean's cousin, for heaven's sake. A flaky, bouncy, sassy, unconventional woman who was about to lose her business unless he allowed her to keep it. And the payment was a bride of his own—not a toss in the hay with Sunny. Though he was tempted.

If he didn't think Sean might kill him, maybe he'd make a play for her—just to while away the time until he found his bride.

It was a pipe dream. He wasn't the type to take advantage of a woman, no matter how tempting she proved.

But for a few seconds, he let his imagination roll.

"Hang on," he growled, angry at himself for the salacious thoughts that pooled in his mind and for the traitorous reaction of his body. They roared out into Chestnut Street. Heading for the beach, he prudently kept to the speed limit.

"This is great," Sunny said in his left ear.

"I thought we'd go down Highway One to Half Moon Bay then cut over. It's a pretty drive along the ocean."

"Great."

She snuggled closer and they were off.

Tanner never had a trip fly by so fast. He alternated between keeping track of the traffic on the road, and imaging pulling off somewhere and kissing the daylights out of his passenger.

He pushed the big bike to the limit, swooping on the curves, opening the throttle on the straightaway—yet always keeping the machine under strict control. He wouldn't take any chances with Sunny's safety. She could trust him in that matter.

And in the other, too. She wasn't his type. She wanted love and devotion and everlasting happiness when she committed to a man. He knew that kind of emotion didn't exist for him, but he could offer stability and respect to the woman he married.

He'd have to find someone for whom that would be enough. Someone who'd advance his social standing, assure his continued access to the important families in San Francisco.

Sunny might be fun for a few days, but she was neither sophisticated nor sleek. More rounded and soft, and—

And it didn't matter a bit. She wasn't what he wanted.

When Sunny said something, Tanner turned his head a bit, trying to hear her.

"What?"

"It's hard to talk," she yelled.

He nodded.

"I thought we were going to discuss my loan."

He shrugged, liking the way her body moved against his.

"We'll have to talk later."

"Not at the picnic. Aunt Patty won't allow business discussions at her parties. We'll have to mingle with everyone there. Maybe this wasn't such a good idea," she said.

"Why not?"

"I don't want to give anyone the wrong impression."

"Tell them we're friends."

"You're friends with Sean. We hardly know each other."

"I don't know, after the other evening in your apartment, I know quite a bit about you. Your favorite color is pink. You like Louis L'Amour books. You hate tomatoes—"

"This is not a date," she yelled.

"How was your date Friday night?" he asked, reminded by her comment.

"Fine."

He waited. Usually Sunny talked thirty words to his one. She had little to say on this subject, however. Was it because the date had been wonderful and none of his business? Or had it been the date from hell and she didn't want to talk about it?

"Care to elaborate?" he asked when she remained silent.

He felt her shake her head against his back.

"I don't kiss and tell," she said primly.

Jealousy pricked him. He tightened his hands in frustration. *She kissed the guy?* Who was he and what did he mean to her?

"Glad to hear that, in case we ever want to try it," he ground out, wanting to find the man and beat him silly.

He still remembered a few tricks from his youth. He felt her shift against him.

"I don't think that would be a good idea," she said.

It would be a dumb idea, he thought. The last thing he needed was any involvement with a woman bent on romance and happy-ever-after. But he couldn't help thinking about her body wrapped around his and her lips on his own. She wouldn't kiss and tell, and he wouldn't, either. But he bet there would be plenty to brag about if they ever did.

Tanner knew the way to the Murphys' house and didn't need Sunny's pointing out where to turn. But he kept quiet, letting her give the direction. He hadn't visited Sean's parents' home in over a decade, but it looked as he remembered when they arrived.

The gardener kept the plants trimmed and controlled. The lawn was a pristine green, manicured within an inch of its life. The old stone house looked fresh and clean with its windows sparkling in the sun.

Tanner pulled into the driveway, maneuvering around the cars already parked along its length and wound his way up near the house. Stopping, he cut the engine. He took off his helmet and shook his head, feeling the breeze blow through his damp hair.

It was warmer here on the peninsula than in the city. The tall trees near the house and behind it would offer much needed shade.

"That was great," Sunny said.

She reached around him and offered her helmet.

"I can't wait for the ride home. We'll have to leave before it gets cold, though," she said.

Holding on to Tanner's shoulder, she swung her leg over and stood on the ground beside the motorcycle. He rocked the bike back onto its stand and swung his leg over, standing beside Sunny, crowding her a bit. One step and he'd be pressed up against her. But he stayed where he was, watching her as she ran her fingers through her hair, trying to bring some of the spring back after being crushed by the helmet.

His fingers itched to touch that hair, and he gave in to the impulse, reaching up and tangling his hand with hers, until the soft curls curved around his fingers—catching hold just like he'd thought it might.

She went still, staring up at him with her pretty blue eyes, emotions changing as quickly as lightning. Slowly he pulled her closer, his hand tangled in her hair, his eyes holding her gaze as the distance between them narrowed. He'd taste those lips again, and not with a slight brush like the last kiss. This time it'd be hot and wet and deep and long. He would open her mouth and learn her taste and touch. He'd bring that sexy body up against his and make her forget kissing last night's date.

Tanner noticed the flush on her cheeks, the way her lips parted slightly as if she were having trouble breathing. His heart kicked in hard and the desire between them couldn't be hidden. Her heat and his mingled, banished only by the slight breeze that cooled his skin. Slowly he drew her closer.

"Tanner Wright. I thought I recognized that motorcycle. It's good to see you again."

Patty Murphy hurried down the walkway from the front door, a wide smile of welcome on her face.

"And Sunny? I didn't expect you to come with Tanner. Or I guess it's the other way around, isn't it?"

At the sound of the voice, Tanner dropped his hand and took two steps back. Standing to his full six feet two inches, he took a deep breath. Two seconds later and Patty Murphy would have found her niece locked in his arms.

"Patty, good to see you again."

He held out his hand, but she brushed it aside and gave him a quick hug. Then holding his arms like he was her son, she studied him.

"Let me look at you. It's been years since I've seen you. Sean keeps me up-to-date, and of course we read about you all the time in the paper. You look tired."

"That's because he works all the time and never takes time

off for recreation, to pump up the creative juices. I told him that he should keep regular hours," Sunny said.

She kept her aunt between her and Tanner and by the nervous way she wiped her hands on her hips, Tanner knew she'd been disturbed by their close call. He smiled grimly. It wasn't over. He'd kiss her before the day was done.

"I'm working on that," he said, nailing her with his gaze.

"We're working on it, wouldn't you say?" Sunny challenged.

"Something I should know about?" Patty asked, picking up on the undercurrents.

"Tanner's advising me on my business. We were supposed to discuss it on the way down, but it's hard to carry a conversation on a motorcycle."

"Or when you can't get a word in edgewise," Tanner murmured.

Patty laughed.

"Sunny does tend to rattle on, doesn't she? Come on, you two, let's get into the backyard. Sean's here and Myra and Becky. I expect your folks will be here before long, Sunny."

"We came early to help set up, if you need it," she said, walking up the walkway, every once in a while throwing a nervous glance toward Tanner.

"I can use the help. Tanner, go on through and see what Sean needs. You come with me, Sunny."

Tanner nodded and headed for the backyard. Though it'd been years since he'd visited, nothing had changed.

"I wonder if I could get the same results trying to boss him around," Sunny said, deliberately loud enough for him to hear as he cut through the family room out to the patio.

Tanner swung around and caught her making a face at his back.

"Want to try?"

He raised one eyebrow.

She opened her mouth as if to meet his challenge, then shook her head and hurried after her aunt.

He watched her go, an easy sight in those tight jeans and top that hugged her figure.

"Hey, Tanner, what are you doing here? Good to see you."

Sean joined him at the door.

"I brought Sunny."

Sean's surprise was almost comical.

"You brought Sunny? What's going on?"

"We had some business to discuss. I couldn't make it yesterday. She suggested we do it today."

Tanner didn't often explain things to others. He'd passed that stage years ago and saw no reason to start with Sean.

"I see," Sean replied, clearly puzzled. "You two strike a deal?"

"She introduced me to Carmella Randolph on Friday."

"Good."

"Not so good. Carmella isn't what I'm looking for. Do you know a Joseph Thurmond Sanger the Fourth?"

"Joe? Sure, his family and ours have known each other for years. Why? Did you come across him recently?"

"What does he do?"

Tanner had no intentions of telling Sean why he wanted to know. He could put one of his employees on the trail, but maybe Sean would offer a shortcut.

"He's a doctor. Works at Seton Medical."

Sean's father joined the two men, greeting Tanner and catching up on business and the subject of Joseph Thurmond Sanger was dropped. But Tanner knew a bit more than when he'd started. For the rest, he'd find out one way or the other. Starting with Sunny.

4

Mid afternoon Tanner grabbed a glass of iced tea from the picnic table and dragged an Adirondack chair into the shade near the patio. Settling in it, he let his gaze wander around the yard. It was crowded with friends and family of the Murphys.

He'd met everyone and remembered each person. It paid to remember names—he'd learned that when he first started in business. Some of today's guests he'd known from when he had visited Sean during college. Others were new to him—like the Quackenbushes.

Sunny's mother was very much like Patty, likable and friendly. Theo Quackenbush obviously adored her and his stepdaughter.

Tanner took a long pull of the tea. He'd helped set things up, kidding with Sean and his father. He'd carried out platters of food for guests to nibble on until time for the barbecue dinner. And unable to help himself, he'd met every new arrival wondering if it would be Joseph Thurmond Sanger the Fourth.

At one point, unable to stand the suspense, he asked Sean if the man was expected. Mixed emotions met Sean's explanation that Joe had to work. Would he have come if he hadn't? Would Sunny have attended the party with Joe instead of himself if the doctor hadn't been on call?

And if he had?

Tanner had no claim on Sunny. She'd invited him because she thought they'd discuss her financial records on the drive down. It didn't matter. She'd invited him. And he was here, not Joseph Thurmond Sanger the Fourth.

Tanner was the man who would take her home tonight. And get some answers about what the other man meant to Sunny.

The emotion that churned in his chest suspiciously resembled jealousy.

Patty and Steve had welcomed him like an old friend, questioning him earlier about what he'd been doing since they last saw him and offered sincere congratulations to his success.

"He likes being top dog," Sunny said in passing.

Her friendly, sunny disposition could almost be construed as flirting. But she was friendly to everyone, even the man threatening to take away her business.

As the afternoon wore on, Tanner felt more and more like an outsider. The other guests played tennis on the court at the end of the lawn or horseshoes on the far side. The children frolicked in the free-form pool, screaming and yelling their delight with the day.

He watched almost enviously. It was a far cry from his own childhood. A far cry from the way some of the boys he knew from Big Brother lived now. Wouldn't they give their back teeth to enjoy such an afternoon?

He made a mental note to explore taking some of the older boys swimming the next time he went.

"Too much?" Sunny asked, dragging a wooden chair over

and plopping down beside him, stretching her legs out before her.

One glance confirmed she'd long ago discarded her shoes.

"Too much what?" he asked, turning slightly so he could see her.

He'd watched her since they arrived, still aware of the kiss they'd almost exchanged, still wanting it. She'd greeted everyone with a hug or a kiss, asked about what was going on, listening with every evidence of fascinated interest. Maybe he should go out and come in. That would get him a hug at least.

"Too much noise, commotion, racket. I don't know. It can get overwhelming sometimes, I think. Maybe not for the parents of the children, they're used to chaos, but the rest of us are more sedate in our activities. This is pure unleashed exuberance. Can you imagine starting your morning early, running everywhere, screaming at the top of your voice, and then having enough energy to go swimming?"

He nodded, smiling slightly.

"Somehow sedate is not an adjective I would normally associate with you."

She laughed.

"Well, maybe sedate isn't the right word. But I wondered if you were looking for an escape. Though I guess you'd walk through the house and out the front door if you were."

He raised an eyebrow. "Oh?"

She nodded, her eyes dancing.

"Sure. I can see you intimidating everybody, never having a qualm about doing whatever you feel like doing at the time."

"Based on your vast knowledge of me."

"Based on your arrogant, don't-give-a-damn attitude,

most of the time," she replied easily. "Actually, I doubt if anyone would even notice for a while. There must be seventy-five people here. Aunt Patty loves to have friends and family over. I think she should have had a dozen babies instead of only Sean and Gloria. Of course if she'd had more boys like Sean, I'm not sure the rest of the world would have survived."

"Sean is a friend of mine," he reminded her lazily.

"And mine, now," she promptly returned. "But I can remember him from when I was a kid and he was a terror. He's almost ten years older than I am. He should have been taking care of me, not driving me crazy. Of course, he's mellowed with age."

"He's not that old."

She looked directly at Tanner, her smile caused him to catch his breath. He wanted to kiss her, here, now, and forget about the crowd in the yard, the women gossiping, the men bragging. What would they all say if he reached out and dragged Sunny into his lap and covered that sassy mouth with his own?

"Why, Tanner Wright, I do declare, I plumb forgot that you're as old as Sean. Of course that puts you right in your prime, isn't that what you said?" she teased.

"Someone should have paddled your backside when you were little."

Laughing again, she studied him, amusement evident.

"Lighten up, Tanner. This is a fun-filled afternoon and here you sit on the sidelines, watching instead of participating. Or are you planning your own parties when you marry that paragon of sophistication that we're going to find you? I'm sure Aunt Patty isn't the least bit concerned with being sophisticated. But are you enjoying today or would you rather we all dressed up and sat quietly sipping white wine?"

"If I marry, it doesn't follow that I will move to Woodside. I like living in the city."

"Ah, but don't you want a huge yard for your kids to roam around in? I expect you'd want them to have every advantage—learn tennis and riding, swimming and dance. Golf lessons at the country club. Fess up, you plan to give them everything money can buy, don't you?"

"Are you badgering my favorite boy?" Patty Murphy asked as she strolled over to join them.

"Whoa, Aunt Patty, what about Sean?" Sunny asked, patting the arm of her chair for her aunt to use.

"Well, he can be a bit tiresome, but Tanner was always the perfect guest. We've missed seeing you these last few years," Patty said, perching on the arm of Sunny's chair. "You don't have to wait for an invitation, nor for Sean to bring you. Stop by sometime and keep us up-to-date with your life."

Tanner nodded, but remained uncommitted.

He'd always felt the welcome from Sean's parents, and always made every effort not to abuse their hospitality. He was too conscious of the vast difference in their backgrounds.

Not that they had ever hinted at any disparities. The visits he'd made when in college had whetted his appetite for the finer things. Their house was warm and welcoming, even with its understated wealth. It was the kind of home he wanted. But ever conscious of his background, he wouldn't intrude.

"Good luck, Aunt Patty. The man works all the time. If I want to call him, I know now to try work first. Even if it's nine o'clock at night. Honestly, he needs a keeper."

"What are you doing calling him at nine at night?" her aunt asked, clearly intrigued.

Sunny blushed.

Tanner watched, fascinated, as the color rose from her throat, flooding into her cheeks, tinting them the most delightful shade of pink. This was the twenty-first century—it was common for women to call men.

Yet the embarrassment was clear. Was there a hint of old-fashioned values in Miss Sunny Pritchard? He grew even more interested in this complex woman.

"Actually, it was business," Sunny mumbled.

"Business?" Patty asked, glancing between the two of them.

"I'm taking a look at her books," Tanner explained, unaccustomed to the surge of protective instinct. "I asked her for some more information and she tried to reach me at home, only trying the office as a last effort."

He threw away the words, as if they meant nothing. No point in getting Patty Murphy thinking anything was going on between them. Especially when there was not.

"And what were you doing there at nine? Don't tell me you are turning into a workaholic. There is too much else to enjoy about life," Patty admonished.

"I enjoy my work," Tanner said, torn between amusement and amazement that Patty seemed to be scolding him.

"I love my work, but know enough that it will be there the next morning. I leave it behind and return refreshed the next morning. If you work constantly, you get used up," Sunny said. "You need a hobby."

His eyebrow rose again. "Such as?"

"I don't know. Want to give horseshoes a try?"

"I'm sure the people who live below me would be thrilled."

She laughed.

"Not at your apartment. Now. The alley is free and we could play. I bet you've never even tried it."

"Go on and give it a shot, Tanner. I'll get Sean to come give you some pointers if you like," Patty said, rising.

Sunny jumped up and reached for Tanner's hand.

"Don't you dare, Aunt Patty. It may be the only time this year I can beat someone at the game. Come on, Tanner, I'll teach you what you need to know."

It was close to dark when Tanner waited by the motorcycle while Sunny finished saying goodbye to everyone. It was later than they'd planned to leave, but after dinner the conversation had been so enjoyable neither of them paid any attention to the time. And it was also growing cool. He had a leather jacket in the bike's compartment, he could let Sunny wear it.

She burst from the front door and ran down the steps.

"Sorry to keep you, I had to talk to Sally Eberhart for a moment. And then Mom insisted I get a sweater for the ride home."

Shrugging into the oversize sweater as she hurried, she continued talking.

"Uncle Steve is lending me this one. It's wool, so supposed to keep me warm even though it's not very thick. Of course I should have told them I could snuggle up to you and keep warm that way, but—"

Her head popped out of the neck and she came to a halt,

gazing straight into Tanner's eyes. He waited for the next bit, wondering what her mother had thought of her snuggling up to him. Knowing he'd enjoy the sensation. Maybe he should yank that sweater off and let her put plan two into action.

"You can snuggle anytime you want," he offered.

She swallowed and licked her lips. He wanted to taste those lips, to feel that delightfully feminine body press against his. To draw her close and capture her energy, hold it for as long as he could.

"Just on the ride home, thanks."

She seemed flustered and he smiled in grim satisfaction. She jarred him off center, time it happened to her. He pulled on his jacket, glad for its warmth. As he kicked the bike off its stand, he thought about their game of horseshoes.

She'd laughed and cheered when she scored, muttered dire imprecations when he did. Yet he couldn't remember another time he'd enjoyed an afternoon so much. She'd drawn him in and banished the feeling of being outside, never giving him another opportunity to sit alone on the sidelines.

It was a gift she shared with her aunt. He wondered if she knew how rare it was.

They rode straight up Highway 280 into the city, skirting the neighborhoods and shopping centers along the way. The lights of San Francisco glittered in the early autumn night, illuminating the tall buildings that soared against the black sky.

"I love the city at night," she said as they rounded the curve and it lay before them, the Bay Bridge outlined in white lights to their right. "It looks like a fairy-tale place, doesn't it?" she said in his left ear.

"Looks like downtown to me."

"That's romantic."

He laughed. The woman was in for a rude awakening if she thought to ever find a spark of romance in him.

"Do you have time for a quick cappuccino?" Tanner asked as the motorcycle slowed for a stoplight.

He didn't usually stop in these trendy coffee places, but knew women liked them. He'd heard plenty about one near the office from Rachel.

"Sure. It's not that late, and I'm still keyed up from the party. Doesn't Aunt Patty throw wonderful ones? I haven't laughed so much since the last one she gave. But I don't think I could have stood much more of Bobby and Stephie Jenkins. If they had argued over one more thing, I would have gone screaming into the night."

Tanner chuckled, remembering the two teenage siblings who couldn't agree on anything. If he had a sister or brother, would they bickered constantly? Or be close, like Sean and his sister? He'd never know.

The coffeehouse was quiet, only a few customers scattered at the small tables. He ordered cappuccino for both of them and followed Sunny to a table near the back wall. It was isolated and quiet. A restful respite after the hectic afternoon.

"We never did get to talk about my business. I loved riding on your motorcycle. Can you believe I'm twenty-six and never rode a motorcycle before? It was so much fun, I might be tempted to get one myself. But practically speaking, if you'd driven a car we could have discussed what your accountant discovered while we rode. I mean, that is why you came with me today, right?"

Tanner stalled by taking a sip of the hot coffee. He couldn't remember why he'd said yes to her invitation, only that he had wanted to spend the day with her. The books were only the excuse he'd used. Not that he'd admit that to anyone.

"I have questions and comments Stuart jotted down. We'll have to make time to go over everything. And I still need your checkbook, to balance the account."

"Let me check my calendar and get back to you. Maybe we could do lunch," she teased, taking a sip of the fragrant coffee. "Mmm. This is so good. You did get decaf, didn't you? I can't be up all night and I'm wired enough from today that it'll be hours before I can sleep as it is. Anyway, I have some work to do when we get home. I thought we'd be back earlier. But at least I have enough energy to get going. It's sample favors for a wedding I'm planning. Sometimes having the actual product for the bride-to-be to hold in her hand helps in the sale."

"I ordered decaf."

"Thanks. I should have known you would. You strike me as the type to do exactly what you say every time. Did you have a good time today?" she asked.

"I did."

Blinking, she grinned. "Careful, Mr. Wright, you might spend a few more words than you can afford. That's it—I did? Would you care to elaborate on what you enjoyed the most? Was it the food, the man-talk by the barbecue pit, or the patter of little feet? Wait, I know. It was learning how to play horseshoes."

"Learning how to try to interpret your version of the rules, you mean. If I thought I'd play again, I'd get a book with the official rules."

But you are what I enjoyed most.

His gaze skimmed over her tousled blond hair, the flush of color on her cheeks, the brightness in her pretty blue eyes. Resting on her lips, he wondered if he would taste the cappuccino if he kissed her now.

He'd wait. They'd be at her apartment soon. Time enough then to indulge in the craving that had surfaced that morning and not yet been assuaged.

"We might not have talked about my financial records, but I came up with another idea of someone for you to meet. Julie Treherne," Sunny said triumphantly.

"Julie Treherne?"

Tanner placed his cup carefully on his saucer and looked up.

"It came to me when we were discussing kids. Julie loves them. And that's a primary reason you want to marry, right? She volunteers at Children's Hospital and works each Christmas on the toys for kids programs. Her mother isn't from the Bay Area, but her father's family came with the gold rush. She might be the perfect choice. And we know she loves kids so she'll be a great mother."

For a moment Tanner hesitated. Why, he refused to consider. He nodded.

"So you can arrange an introduction."

"Same as before, if you like."

"Let me choose the restaurant this time," he said dryly.

"Not into salads and pasta?" she asked, her eyes dancing in amusement.

He wanted to bottle that look, take it home and be able to take it out anytime he wanted to be cheered up. She had such a freshness enthusiasm about her that it made him feel centuries older and eons more cynical.

"I felt like I walked into a garden."

"Okay, we'll try something more masculine. How about the London Pub over on Kearney?"

"When?"

"I'll have to call you once I set something up with Julie."

He took another sip of the fragrant brew.

"Tell me something, Sunny. Do you plan to get married sometime?"

"I hope so. I want what my mother and father had. What Mom found again with Theo."

She flashed her grin and shrugged her shoulders.

"I know, you think I'm hopelessly romantic, but I don't care. I want love so strong I never feel alone again. When it comes, I want to feel bonded for life to one man. And then I want lots of kids. I'm an only child, you know. I loved visiting with Sean and Gloria, even though they're older. They had each other, but I had no brothers or sisters. I wished Mom and Theo had a few, but they never did."

Tanner remembered her brief background Sean had reported. After the death of Sunny's father, it had only been she and her mother for a number of years. They shared that bit of similarity, though she didn't know it. Only her childhood had taken a turn for the better when Theo Quackenbush married her mother. His had continued, solitary, lonely, poor. No new mother came into their home, it had been only he and his father.

"So what will you do with your dozens of kids?" he asked, shaking off the gloom of memories.

"Cut back on work, for one thing. I missed my mother so much when she had to go to work after Daddy died. So I'd arrange for Eve or someone else to take on more responsibility and I'd spend time with my children. We'd go whale watching in spring, and to the zoo. Did you know sometimes you can get a night pass and go in after dark? All the animals look different after dark. It's spooky, but a lot of fun—as long as you remember a flashlight. Then we could go backpacking in Yosemite or explore all the little shops in Chinatown."

"And would you send them to the school you attended?"

Sunny wrinkled her nose.

"Probably not. It was fine and Theo really wanted me to go there. Mom had gone and Aunt Patty and Theo's sister, so it was sort of a tradition. And I got a good education. But I also enjoyed the local public school when I went, probably would have received just as fine an education. Did you go to private school?"

He shook his head, dark amusement lurking.

"About as far from some fancy private school as you can get," he answered, memories of his high school days not something he cared to dwell upon.

"There, see, you turned out fine. I think San Francisco has a great public school system, so my kids would go there."

She looked up from beneath her lashes and held his gaze, hers teasing.

"I don't think our kids would interact too often, would they? I don't plan on lessons on every activity from ballet to archery. I don't plan on some ritzy, snooty private school. If they want to learn something, I'll be supportive, but I'm not one for forcing things down people's throats and especially not a child's."

"I want more for my children than I had," Tanner said. "I want to offer them the best that money can buy. I have the resources and plan to use them. No child of mine will ever want for anything."

She blinked and stared at him.

"Excuse me? You sound like you plan to buy your children everything they ever ask for."

"Right."

"Great way to spoil them and have them grow up expecting the world at their feet. Which it won't be."

"They'll be mine to spoil. I can afford to buy anything."

"Tanner, children don't need lots of *things*. They just need love. A child will develop into a far better adult if he has love and attention from his parents. A strong home so he'll know he's safe and wanted and loved. Toys and such are fine for treats or special events, but you sound as if you plan to throw things his way."

"Of course he'd have attention. My wife won't work, she'll stay home with the children. I'll be home nights and weekends."

"You'll have to change your habits," she murmured.

"Think I wouldn't?"

"I guess you would, if that was what you wanted. I have to get home now. This has been a wonderful day. Thank you for coming to Aunt Patty's with me."

He rose and reached for her hand, lacing his fingers through hers. Her skin was soft, her fingers strong, yet small when compared with his. She didn't pull away, but held on as if holding hands was something they always did.

For the first time Tanner wondered what it would be like to be friends with Sunny Pritchard. Forget about his threat of foreclosing on her business, forget about her finding him a bride, just take the time they had together to enjoy. He'd never had a woman friend, and wasn't sure it was possible. But for a moment he was willing to try.

"So I'll check with Julie and call you. Any day this week okay with you?" she chattered as they headed for the bike.

"If I see a conflict, I'll call you."

"Okay. I'll try for early in the week."

When Tanner reached her apartment house, she slid off the bike before he cut the engine.

"Thanks for taking me today."

She held out her helmet.

"I'll walk you to your door," he said, removing the key and snapping off his helmet.

"I'm sure I'll be fine."

"Probably, but I'll still walk you to your door."

Somewhere between the coffee shop and her apartment, her warmth had cooled. He didn't try to reach for her hand, but quietly followed her up the steps in the old building to the second floor. Waiting patiently while she fished out keys from her snug jeans, he resisted the urge to sweep her into his arms and kiss her until morning.

"About your finances—" he said.

She glanced up warily, and looked adorable. Unable to resist temptation that had plagued him all day, he reached out and cupped her chin in one hand, lowering his face until her sweet breath brushed across his cheeks.

"What about them?"

Her eyes deepened in color, and a hint of pink swamped her cheeks. Tanner liked the effect. He wondered how often he could provoke a blush.

"We need to spend some time together to review them. How about one night this week?"

"Fine. You're the one who stays at work until all hours. I normally leave around five or six."

"I'll call you."

He leaned forward the scant inch that separated them and closed his lips over hers. He slid his hand around until it cradled her head, his fingers tangling in the soft silky hair. The starch evaporated and Sunny made a soft sound in the back of her throat as she leaned against him, her fingers clutching his arms.

He deepened the kiss, holding her close, reveling in the sweet sensation of their embrace. Endless moments ticked by as they were lost in a world of sensuous haze and delight. Slowly reality returned.

Tanner ended the kiss, resting his forehead against hers as he looked into her bemused eyes.

"I'll call you," he repeated.

"Okay. You do that." She licked her lips, looking stunned. "I'll be home most nights. So whenever..."

Her voice trailed off and she moved one finger to trace his lips, pulling back to see him clearly.

"I'm not sure kissing me is getting much accomplished."

He released her.

"What do you want to accomplish?"

"Finding you a wife so you'll back off foreclosing on my business."

He stepped back, feeling as if he'd been slapped.

"I haven't forgotten our agreement, Sunny. You do your part and I'll live up to mine."

Without another word, he turned and left.

Seething at the way she'd changed the flow of the evening, he wanted to punch something. How dare she complain about their kiss? It was no big deal. Most men expected a kiss after a date. It wasn't as if he pushed her into bed.

Not that the thought didn't come to mind, lurking in the recesses to distract his attention, his focus. He was on a wife hunt and needed Sunny's help. Their relationship was solely business.

So why the anger at her comment? It was nothing but true.

Her purpose now was to introduce him to a possible mate. In exchange, he'd forgive the business loan. It was a sensible arrangement.

So why did her kisses tempt him so much? Why had he considered making an attempt at friendship? Why did he want Sunny so much when she was totally opposite to his picture of an ideal wife? He needed to make sure he remembered their deal and moved ahead.

Sunny didn't impress him with her business acumen, nor speed in closing a deal. Maybe he needed to push her a bit. As soon as he found his ideal bride, he could turn over Sunny's loan papers and move to the next stage of his life.

He sat on the bike and looked up at her windows. The light was on, but the shade drawn. He couldn't see her.

And he couldn't erase the echo of her words. When she

married it would be for love. Nothing less.

He kicked the bike on and eased the throttle. Pulling onto the main street, he opened the throttle and sped toward his own condo in the marina.

Love was an illusion, a fancy term for lust and affection and commitment. He would not be seduced by the illusion.

When he married, it would be with both eyes open, and with a commitment on both parts for a lifetime marriage.

5

Tanner entered the London Pub a few minutes before noon on Tuesday. As promised, Sunny had called and left a message with Rachel that she and Julie would be meeting for lunch today. He arrived a few minutes early, in hopes of spotting them as they came in.

Maybe he could make a snap judgment about this Julie and if she didn't appear to suit, he could forgo lunch with another woman who compared her father's wealth to everything else.

The decor was that of an old English pub. Dark paneled walls polished to a high gloss reflected the brass lamps that hung from the ceiling, which, along with the wall sconces, provided the illumination for the restaurant. The chairs were solid, the tables of dark wood.

Tanner had eaten here a time or two before. He liked the quiet elegance, the quick service and the illusion of privacy. The tables were not crowded one against another to pack in the customers. The owner preferred quality over quantity. And the patrons paid dearly for the dining experience.

He felt a surge of pride that he no longer worried about the cost of things. It was a far cry from the struggling times of his youth.

Scanning the large dining area, he spotted Sunny and a

petite dark-haired woman just taking seats. Obviously they arrived even earlier. Was he typecasting women—thinking they were always late? He frowned. He needed to be able to read people in order to succeed in his business ventures. He didn't want prejudices to interfere.

He started for their table.

"Can I help you, sir?"

The maître d' stepped in front of Tanner, his silver hair gleaming in the muted lighting.

"I am joining the ladies over there."

He nodded toward Sunny's table.

"They made no mention of expecting a third party."

The maitre d' obviously took his role seriously.

Tanner looked at him.

"Sunny Pritchard is the blonde and she is expecting me. Perhaps she neglected to mention the fact when being seated."

Obviously torn, the man hesitated a moment. Then, after a quick glance at Tanner's Armani suit and expensive silk tie, conceded defeat.

Tanner smiled cynically. Look and act the role and people will accept it without question. It was a maxim he'd learned years ago.

"If you will follow me."

The man took off through the tables, his bearing upright and stiff.

Blast it. Tanner didn't want the maitre d' involved. How spontaneous would it look with the man leading him directly to their table?

"Madam, your third party has arrived."

The maître d' stood stiffly by the table, eyeing Tanner as if he were a suspected pickpocket.

"Oh."

Sunny looked up at Tanner, at the maître d', and then cast a quick glance at Julie.

"You've been more than helpful," Tanner growled at the maître d' as he slid out a chair and waited for Tanner to be seated.

"Oh, Tanner. Won't you join us?"

Sunny said, looking at the chair the maître d' held.

Tanner sat down and glared at Sunny. If she had other ideas of how to meet prospective brides, she'd better come up with them fast. This was the last time he'd pull a stupid stunt like this.

"Uh, Julie, I'd like you to meet Tanner Wright, a friend of mine."

Sunny looked flustered. Tanner almost smiled at the picture. Once again he was struck by Sunny's lack of guile and subterfuge. He nodded to the pretty dark-haired woman seated to his left.

"Julie?"

"Julie Treherne, I'm happy to meet you. Were you and Sunny supposed to meet for lunch? If I'm in the way, we can reschedule."

She looked at Sunny, a question in her eyes.

"No, of course not, Julie. I wanted to have lunch with you. I—"

She stared in Tanner in supplication.

"I often eat here, Julie. When I arrived and saw Sunny, I thought I'd stop by and say hello. Our friend at the door didn't seem to understand," Tanner improvised, ruthlessly maligning the maître d'. "I'm really the intruder. If you'd rather, I can sit at another table."

It would probably prove a better idea, he thought, thoroughly disgusted with the entire situation.

"No, of course not, Tanner. Do stay. Will that be all right, Julie?" Sunny said breathlessly.

"Sure. You know I have to leave in a bit, anyway. I'm working this afternoon at the hospital and don't want to be late."

"Right. Julie volunteers at Children's Hospital," Sunny said brightly, her gaze fixed on Tanner.

Some of the worry faded, but she still looked flustered.

He nodded and picked up the menu, striving for some normalcy.

"She loves children," Sunny added.

He flicked her a glance. She looked stressed. Turning to Julie, he smiled politely.

"Have any of your own?" he asked.

Sunny yelped and shook her head, her curls dancing.

"Tanner, Julie isn't married," she explained as if to a two-year-old. She glared at him.

"What a coincidence," he said, holding Sunny's gaze.

He liked her flustered. He didn't remember seeing her like this before.

"I'm not married, either."

"Oh, for goodness sakes."

Sunny rolled her eyes, and reached for a glass of water. Sipping desperately, she looked at Julie.

Tanner also looked at Julie and liked what he saw. She was

dainty and petite. Her hair was glossy black, worn in a casual cut that would be easy to care for. Her clothes were stylish without being ostentatious. And there was not a single piece of jewelry in sight.

He wondered what her father did and if she knew his net worth to the dime.

"Tell me about volunteering at the hospital," he said, taking pity on a decidedly nervous Sunny.

Julie instantly plunged into recounting every experience she'd found working with children. Tanner listened with half an ear as she droned on and on about some child who had proved a terror while in the hospital and how she'd been instrumental in calming him down.

Another about a boy who almost single-handedly wrecked the X-ray equipment until she stepped in to save the day.

Stories of relieving overworked nurses, of rocking fretful babies until they cooed with happiness, of bringing treats and reading stories to the demanding toddlers who depended on her to soothe their stay grew old fast.

He flicked a glance at Sunny. She sat still as stone, a silly grin plastered on her face, her eyes glazed slightly as she kept them firmly fixed on Julie.

Ordering lunch only halted the monologue temporarily. After ten minutes, Tanner mentally apologized to Sunny for ever thinking she talked nonstop. He'd give anything to hear her interpose a few words.

To hear anyone else say something for a few minutes.

Lunch arrived and Julie at last became quiet.

While the silence stretched out, Tanner reviewed his requirements for a wife. Obviously along the way he'd neglected to mention he liked conversation, a give-and-take between adults, not a monologue. He'd have to refine his list.

"Tanner has season tickets to the 49ers," Sunny blurted out.

Both of her table companions stared at her.

"Right?" she asked.

"Yes."

Tanner pressed his lips together to keep from smiling.

Sunny obviously didn't like the quiet that had enveloped the table. What would she say next? While he might enjoy conversation, he had no more patience with inane remarks than monologues.

"Roger works for the 49ers," Julie said.

"Roger?" Tanner asked.

"My cousin, Roger Jackson, he works in the office."

"I didn't know that," Sunny said brightly. "How interesting. Isn't that interesting, Tanner?"

His lips twitched.

"Very interesting."

He laid down his fork and leaned back, watching Sunny, trying to guess what she would do next.

"Uh, Tanner graduated from Stanford like my cousin Sean."

He almost smiled. Ever the trouper, his Sunny.

"My cousins Beth and Rolly both went to Stanford. Of course Jack and Roger went to Berkeley, so that always causes lively discussions during Big Game Week," Julie replied.

"You seem to have a big family," Tanner commented.

"I guess, let me see..."

Stifling a groan when she started naming the members of

her family and their occupations, Tanner had no one to blame but himself. After her discourse on the hospital, he should have known she'd be able to go all night with her family. And as he tried to keep the names and relations straight, he realized she really did have a large family.

And seemed totally in awe of each one, quoting their words as if they were gems.

At a pause, he pushed back his chair.

"Sorry not to be able to hear about the rest of your clan, Julie, but I have to get back to work."

"Oh, look at the time. I didn't realize. I'll be late at the hospital. They do depend on me so much. I hate to be late. Do you want to share a cab? Sunny, it's been great. We'll have to do it again real soon. I'll call you."

Julie pushed back her chair and stood, smiling at Tanner. Her expression quiet with satisfaction, Sunny looked from one to the other.

"Lunch sometime would be fine."

Tanner didn't like that look.

And if Julie thought by leaving at the same time he'd share anything with her, she was sadly mistaken.

"Sunny, shall I drop by tonight, or would later in the week be better?" Tanner said, moving to her side and leaning over slightly as if implying a degree of intimacy.

Actions spoke louder than words, and as with Carmella, he didn't want Julie to have any wrong ideas about their meeting.

"Tonight?"

Sunny looked blank.

"About eight"

He brushed his lips across hers and straightened.

"I'll walk out with you, Julie, but I don't need a cab. I'm only a couple blocks from my office and can walk."

Reaching his office a few minutes later, Tanner took off his jacket and settled into his chair. He drew the latest figures from the proposed joint venture between rival factions in the Silicon Valley from the stack of folders on his desk.

An awareness of anticipation hummed beneath the surface. He knew from Sunny's shocked expression that she wouldn't ignore his farewell. How long before she called and blasted him to kingdom come?

The door flung open and slammed against the wall. Tanner looked up, and almost smiled. No more phone calls.

"You can't just barge in like that."

Rachel stood beside Sunny as if considering whether dragging the intruder from her boss's office was a possibility. Sunny ignored her, her eyes latching onto Tanner. She stomped across the carpeted floor, fury radiating from every inch of her. Tossing her purse onto a visitor's chair, she glared at Tanner, her hands on her hips.

Tanner placed the prospectus on the desk and nodded at Rachel.

"It's all right, Rachel. I'll deal with this."

Once the door closed behind her, Sunny exploded.

"You'll deal with what? I thought you were serious about trying to find a wife. I've been racking my brains for days trying to come up with that perfect paragon you want and each time I present someone who would suit, you act like a stupid idiot and try to make them think there is something going on between us."

She slammed one fist on his desk. He wondered if it hurt. Her fist wasn't so big and the desk was massive.

"I thought we agreed to pretend the meetings were spontaneous, unexpected. Instead, you have the maître d' come over and say I was expecting you. I couldn't believe it. How can I pretend anything is spontaneous when you are announced like that? We're just lucky Julie left with you instead of staying to cross-examine me."

She paused and took a breath. "Not only that," she continued before he could open his mouth. "I can't believe you kissed me in public. Do you have any idea what kind of impression that would make on Julie? Not only that, but did you know Martin Crawley was sitting two tables away? He's a good friend of Theo's. I can just imagine his comments to my stepfather. 'Say, Theo, old man, didn't know little Sunny was involved with a man.' 'What man?' Theo will ask. And then Steve will tell him about the entire sordid scene and Theo will remember you were at Aunt Patty's and soon the entire family will think there's something between us and we know there 's nothing."

She turned away and stormed to the window.

Tanner watched her, trying to gauge her anger. Was she truly furious or was there something else simmering beneath the surface?

After a moment, she turned and stormed back to the desk.

"Well, aren't you going to say anything?"

He shrugged.

"What's there to say? Julie's not what I'm looking for."

She rolled her eyes and flopped down into the chair across from him.

"A simple 'It was nice to meet you, Julie, goodbye,' would have sufficed, don't you think? But no, you have to go on and deliberately tell her you would be dropping in at my place later. I bet Martin heard that, too. Oh, great. Now my mother will be on me trying to find out why I haven't mentioned you before and getting hurt feelings that she and I are not as close as we once were. When of course we are, because there's nothing to tell about you and me. I certainly don't want the family to know I'm having trouble with the business. They would all jump in and insist I take a loan. I wanted to make it on my own. Darn, darn, darn."

She jumped up.

Tanner looked at her. Was she shorter? Rising slightly, he glanced at her feet. Her shoes were lying on their sides, obviously kicked off.

"Anyway, what's wrong with Julie? She's pretty, very polished, and loves kids. The perfect mate. Or as perfect as you're likely to get."

He leaned back in his chair and watched her pace his office. Her eyes were darker than he'd ever seen them. Her cheeks a rosy blush of anger that caught his eye. He wondered if her skin felt warmer with that color.

Wondered if he could kiss her out of her anger.

Not likely.

"First, Julie is pretty, but a bit short for me, don't you think?" he asked calmly, belying the increased heart rate as he watched her turn and walk back toward him.

"How short is too short? She's not much shorter than I am. Am I too short? You never mentioned anything about short or tall. I thought you wanted sophisticated and impeccable bloodlines. You never mentioned height as a requirement. I would have remembered if you had."

Sunny was just the right size, he thought whimsically. The top of her head came to just above his shoulder. He had to lean over a bit to kiss her, but when he'd pulled her into his arms, she fit perfectly.

"I want sophisticated, but a certain height would be preferred. Do you want me to get a permanent backache leaning over to kiss my wife the rest of my life?"

She frowned, staring at him as if something unexpected had been said. Taking a breath, she looked away.

"That's it? You're afraid of backaches?"

"No. Did you notice how every story she told about the hospital reflected on how wonderful she was to be volunteering? What a heroine she is in every scenario? I wonder how the place runs without her," he said dryly.

Sunny looked out of the expanse of windows. Slowly she walked over to them and leaned against the sill, gazing at San Francisco. Tanner thought he caught a glimpse of a smile in her reflection.

"You're right. She did come across as the heroine of every event. But at least she likes children. Family's important to her. I thought you wanted that."

"She sounds as if she's related to half of the city. And if she quoted one more relative, I would have gone crazy. Doesn't she have an original thought in her own mind?"

Sunny looked at him over her shoulder.

"I thought men liked that, having the woman parrot their every thought as if they were a god or something."

"If a man's looking for a life partner, he wants someone

who can think for herself. Otherwise, it'd be like talking to myself. And that's another thing. She talks nonstop."

Sunny smiled at that.

Tanner felt the now familiar clutch at her lopsided grin and his entire office brightened. It was as if sunshine invaded the somber room.

Slowly he rose and crossed the room to stand beside her by the bank of windows.

"She did tend to get carried away. Maybe she was nervous. You are rather an intimidating presence," she said.

"I've never noticed you are particularly intimidated."

"Well, you're a friend of Sean's. Almost a cousin, you could say."

"Don't start listing all your relatives and quoting them," he warned.

She laughed.

"Don't try to turn the subject, Tanner. I'm still mad at you."

"Why?"

"For one thing, you didn't give Julie a chance. I think she's just what you're looking for. She'll make a good wife and wouldn't want to work. She loves her volunteer job. Working around that when the kids come would be an asset."

"I didn't like the way she bragged about it. I volunteer but don't have to make myself the center of attention."

"You do? Where?"

Clearly intrigued, Sunny turned to face him, her face alive with curiosity.

He frowned. He hadn't meant to say that. Few people

knew about his activities with the center and it suited him to keep it that way.

"Tanner, where do you volunteer?"

Her hand came out and touched his arm. He could feel the heat through the fine cotton of his shirt. Slowly he looked at her. She was waiting patiently, a decided contrast to the rampant curiosity that blazed in her eyes.

"We are discussing Julie Treherne, not my personal life," he said coldly.

"We'll discuss Julie in a minute. Right now I want to know where you volunteer. Is it with old people, children, the sick? I can't believe this. Most men like you say they have too little time to volunteer regularly. Oh, I suspect that's what you meant. Especially in the same sentence with talking about Julie's regular schedule."

"Let it go, Sunny."

"I won't. Tell me."

He hesitated, then nodded once.

"I help out at a Big Brothers center for boys in the Tenderloin—a couple of Saturdays a month. It's not such a big deal."

"The Tenderloin? You actually go into the Tenderloin?"

She couldn't have expressed any more surprise if he'd told her it was on the moon.

The Tenderloin was one of the poorest sections of San Francisco. There were stories of gangs and shootings and drugs. As far from the elegant surroundings of his Montgomery Street office as she could possibly imagine.

"Why in the world do you volunteer there? There are other boys' clubs in safer neighborhoods."

He nodded, once.

"How in the world did you even find out about the center, much less get started working there?"

Sunny was clearly baffled.

Tanner wondered if she were trying to envision her cousin Sean or some of her friends doing that. Impossible, probably.

He smiled grimly.

"I am from the Tenderloin. It was sort of like going home."

She stared at him, dropped her gaze to his expensive shirt, the costly tie, the discrete gold watch at his wrist. Slowly her gaze moved back up until it collided with his own.

"Not fit the image you had?" he asked.

For some reason her answer was important.

"How long did you live there?" she asked.

"How long? I grew up there, Sunny. My old man was a dock worker, when he could stay sober enough to work. Otherwise he took whatever odd jobs he could to keep us in food and liquor. I left when I won the scholarship to Stanford."

"And never looked back."

"My father's dead. My mother left when I was little. No need to look back."

"But you go there now to volunteer?"

"You wouldn't understand."

"I might. In fact, I bet I do. You had a...a sparse childhood, and now you have a ton of money. You want to do something for the kids still living there."

"Sparse?"

He laughed, shook his head.

"Only you would call abject poverty *sparse*. But I was lucky, I got out. Now I'm trying to make sure some of the others can get out, too."

"I doubt it was luck. You seem to make your own luck. And I'd say hard work and lots of studying got you into Stanford. And got you where you are today. But it sure explains your demands for a high-society wife. You can't erase the past by marrying into some other family."

"So my roots will always show?" He raised one eyebrow, narrowing his eyes. "What are you trying to say—that I'm not good enough for the fancy wife I want?"

"No, I didn't mean that."

She looked horrified.

"I meant, finding the bloodlines you want isn't everything. You should be tremendously proud of all you've accomplished. I know you want to leave your fortune to a son, but don't shortchange yourself in the process. Don't marry only to make sure your son would never end up in the Tenderloin. What about you? Don't you want more? You should hold out for love."

"Oh, no, don't give me that. I know you think love surrounds everyone and maybe it does surround you. Or maybe you see things in such rose-colored glasses that you can believe in such nonsense. But in real life, I'm not sure it even exists and I don't plan to live my entire life searching for something that doesn't exist."

"Your way of finding a wife is so cold-blooded."

"But it is my way and it suits me. I don't want my son to be ashamed of his father, or long for a mother he never knew. I want him surrounded by stability and financial security.

Marriage is a merger of two lives and something to be entered coolly and logically. We wouldn't have so many divorces today if everyone took a bit more time to fully consider every aspect before getting married. The illusion of love doesn't last."

"I don't believe that."

She sighed, and looked back out the window.

"I'm not sure I can help you."

"You'll help me or lose Brides and Bows."

A split second of panic touched him before he snapped out the words. They had a deal and everyone knew he held all participants to every term of a deal. Was she attempting to renege?

"You have to do your part. Maybe you should invite Julie on a date."

"Give it up, Sunny. If I couldn't stand lunch with the woman, there's no way I'm going to want to spend the rest of my life with her."

"Just what do you want? I've introduced you to two people I thought would work, based on your list of requirements. Both are pretty, stylish, rich, come from San Francisco's finest families. Neither work, both would stay home with your children. Both would be an asset in spending your money. What else?"

"I don't know. There's just something missing."

Maybe it was that neither woman brought sunshine into his life. He was aware of Sunny, standing inches away. Her scent wafted gently in the air, teasing his nostrils. She stood in her stocking feet, her softly draped blouse concealing as much as it revealed. The long light wool pants did nothing to remind him of her jeans on Sunday. He rather thought he liked the snug jeans better.

"You might have to ease up on some of your requirements," she said slowly.

"Like what?"

"I know some women whom you might like, but they work. And I can't call them up and ask them if they plan to work once they have children. But if it comes up in the conversation, I'll pass it along."

She tilted her head and stared up at him.

"Want to give that a try?"

Her expression was wistful, her eyes deep and luminous and mesmerizing. He felt he could stare into her eyes all day.

Except he'd rather kiss her.

Without further thought, he leaned across the distance that separated them and did just that.

She didn't move. Didn't step closer, didn't pull away. For endless moments his lips caressed hers and she responded. Then Tanner straightened.

"What was that for?"

Her voice sounded throaty, soft, bemused. Almost caressing, he thought in disgust.

This deal was unlike any other business venture. Was he getting soft in his old age? Next time he'd stick to businessmen who dealt in dollars and cents, not soft women with rosy views of life and silky skin that tantalized and taunted him to touch, to feel, to taste.

"Friends?" he offered.

The idea of being friends grew with every meeting. Of being more than friends.

She blinked and drew in a deep breath.

"I guess."

"I don't want to meet for lunch with the next candidate."

"What then? That is so easy."

"You can think of something, I'm sure."

"If you want, I could fix you up with someone and not be there. A blind date?"

"No. You have to be there. If I need an out, I can use you."

"Fine, use me then. But unless I give a party or something, I don't know of many ways to be in the midst of an introduction. Oh, wait, I know of a party. I received the invitation a couple of weeks ago. I wasn't going, but maybe that'd be the answer. You can come as my date. I'll introduce you to everyone and you can decide who you want. Why didn't I think of this earlier? It would get it all over with at once. It's Toddy and Denise's anniversary party. Practically everyone we went to school with will be there, married and singles alike. As will a range of other people. They always have hordes attending. It's perfect. It's a week from Saturday."

"I volunteer at the center on Saturdays."

"It doesn't start until seven or eight at night. You can work all day at your boys' center and then party all night. I'll have to scrounge around for the invitation. I don't remember what I did with it. I hadn't planned on going. But it would be the perfect opportunity for you to meet several women at once. As soon as I find it, I'll call you and let you know the details. This is perfect."

Tanner considered the alternatives. He wasn't much for parties, but it was a way to meet women without giving rise to unrealistic expectations.

"All right."

"But this is the last try. You have to find someone from this group. I don't know anyone else," she warned.

"Then I'd better fulfill my part of the bargain. Did you want me to come by tonight to go over your records?"

"Oh, I forgot."

She turned and hurried to her purse, which she had tossed in the chair. Rummaging in it for a couple of seconds, she waved a checkbook triumphantly.

"I remembered. I meant to give it to you at lunch, but forgot with everything else that was going on."

He took it from her and slapped it against the palm of one hand.

"Tonight, Sunny?"

"I won't be home tonight. Besides, you need to look at the checkbook first, don't you?"

"Why won't you be home?"

Everything inside him went still. Was she going out on a date?

"I'm meeting Joe for pizza and a movie. We're going to see that new adventure flick. Why is it guys love adventure movies? You'd think a doctor would be tired of all the blood and violence, but Joe loves them."

"Joseph Thurmond Sanger the Fourth," Tanner murmured, clamping down on the emotion that started to swell.

She was free to date whomever she wished. But why did he hate hearing about it? The emotion churning inside threatened to consume him. She looked at him warily.

"Mostly we call him Joe."

"Blue blood from way back?" he asked silkily.

Nodding cautiously, she watched him as he stepped closer.

"I guess you could say so. His family came to California generations ago and has always been very prominent in San Francisco politics. His uncle was the mayor a few years back. He doesn't have a sister, if that's what you're hinting at. Only two brothers. I don't even think he has any female cousins."

"Why are you going out with him?"

Why did he care? Sunny wasn't his type. He wanted sophisticated and savvy, not a romantic with an ingenue enthusiasm. But he didn't like knowing she preferred Joseph Thurmond Sanger over him.

"Why not, we're friends."

She licked her lips, the wariness giving way to confusion. "Just friends?"

He pushed, he wanted to know more about this relationship, needed to know more. Did Joe kiss her? Did she like his kisses? Want more? Jealousy burned deep in Tanner as he awaited her answer.

She nodded.

"How friendly?"

He reached out and captured one of her curls, smoothing it around his finger, his thumb registering the soft texture.

"Friends. You know, someone to do something with."

"Are we friends, Sunny? We did something together Sunday, going to the barbecue."

"Friends don't blackmail other friends into helping them," she snapped instantly.

He smiled slowly.

"Our deal isn't blackmail, it's business. I'm talking about

being friends. I've never had a woman for a friend before."

"Somehow I'm not surprised."

She licked her lips again, her eyes darting from his to his mouth.

"Sunny, I want you and me to be friends."

He leaned over and kissed her again. Lightly, not giving in to the need that built inside to crush her against him and kiss her until the sun set, but nonetheless responding to the silent invitation she issued.

"Uh, sure. Tanner. We're friends, I guess," she said when he released her.

Color rose in her cheeks again, but he knew it was not anger this time.

"Spend Saturday with me?"

"I thought you worked at the center in the Tenderloin on Saturdays."

"Every other one. I worked last week, but next Saturday is free. Spend it with me."

He almost demanded she do so, but caution stilled his tongue. He wouldn't force the issue, unless he had to. But if she had time for her *friend* Joseph Thurmond Sanger *the Fourth*, she could as well make time for him.

"Doing what?" she asked, taking a step back.

Reluctantly he let his finger slip from her hair, dropped his hand to his side.

"We can decide when I come to your place tomorrow night."

"What?"

"I still need to go over your books."

6

"You never give up, do you?" Sunny asked, frowning. "Look on it as protecting my investment."

"Your investment? Brides and Bows is *my* boutique."

"And I hold the note on it. If this party is our last shot and nothing turns up, I'll foreclose. Then Brides and Bows will be a part of Wright Associates," Tanner said coolly.

He didn't believe in mixing business with anything.

"I've introduced you to two appropriate women," she protested. "It's not fair that you'll take my business."

"That's what we're discussing, Sunny, business. From a logical point, I've already given you more time and latitude than is justified. My company made you a loan. You have not repaid it. You owe me."

She stuck her feet into her shoes.

"I'm doing the best I can," she muttered, snagging her purse and slipping the strap on her shoulder.

Tossing her head, she faced him from across the office.

"Come at eight. But don't come in a suit or I won't let you in."

"Dictating terms?" he asked softly.

"You're dern tooting. After you have your say about my accounting methods, which I'm sure you'll find a total mess, I want more discussion on the qualities of this wife of your dreams. If the party is my last shot for Brides and Bows, I have to make it a success. Eight o'clock, and no suit."

She made an exit worthy of a stage actress, he thought as he watched her sail from the office. The door almost slammed, but at the last second Sunny apparently had second thoughts. She closed it quietly. The click when the latch engaged sounded loud as he stared after her, torn between amusement and frustration.

He hadn't run the gamut of so many emotions in more than a decade, if ever. Yet around Sunny, he was subjected to a full barrage. He slapped the checkbook against his palm again and wondered why he was willing to put up with so much from her.

If his mother had remained, would his parents have had more children? Would he have had a sister like Sunny? Not at all likely, not living where he'd grown up. Children there acquired a hard edge early. They didn't live with a rosy view of life, they faced reality as babies. Sunny would never survive in such a place. And he hoped she never even visited.

Tanner called Stuart to come for the checkbook and finish his analysis of the records for Brides and Bows. The accountant sighed softly when handed the checkbook but made no comment.

"I want it by tomorrow at five," Tanner said as dismissal.

"No problem, boss. At least I hope not. You'll have everything on your desk before five."

Tanner glanced at his watch. It was scarcely three. He had over twenty-nine hours before he'd see Sunny again. Time he needed to spend on work, not on thinking about a blond fireball who set his emotions churning.

Promptly at eight o'clock the next evening Tanner rang the bell to Sunny's apartment. The door opened a crack and he saw Sunny peek out at him. Smiling broadly, she threw the door wide.

"Hi," she said, her eyes running appreciably down his body, taking in the casual brown slacks he'd worn with the cream pullover shirt.

"Looking good, Mr. Wright," she said, stepping back so he could enter.

"Relaxed enough, Ms. Pritchard?" he asked.

"Admit it, you feel better in those clothes than in a suit and tie."

Not that he'd admit it, but he felt better seeing her. Enough that he'd done as she had requested and worn casual attire–he wasn't going to give her the complete satisfaction of agreeing with her.

"Ready for business?" he asked.

Sighing, Sunny nodded, motioning to the small alcove where she had her dining room table and chairs.

"I thought we could spread everything out on the table and you can lecture me on basic accounting."

"Lecture?"

He raised an eyebrow.

She eyed him through lowered lashes.

"Isn't that the purpose of this? I can't imagine my record-keeping is up to your usual standard."

"Let's just say you have an innovative and creative way with accounting like you do with your bridal dresses."

She smiled.

"Sit. Can I get you some coffee?"

"If it's strong and black."

"All the better to keep us awake while we go over this?"

"Does accounting bore you, Sunny?"

From the table, he could see her bustle around in her small kitchen. He wondered how good a cook she was and if she entertained often. That thought brought others—ones he didn't care for.

"How was your date with Joseph Thurmond Sanger the Fourth last night?" he asked.

Her head swung around and she stared at him for the longest time. Slowly her eyes narrowed. Picking up the cups, she approached the table.

"You know, you could just call him Joe like the rest of us," she said slowly.

Placing his cup before him, she pulled back the chair to his right and plunked down.

"My date was fine," she said.

"Where did you go?"

"Good grief, you sound like a jealous husband. We went for pizza saw a movie. We had fun. End of discussion. You didn't come here tonight to grill me on my date with Joe, did you?"

He shook his head, wondering if he were lying to himself. He didn't like the thought of Sunny out with another man. Refusing to dwell on the precise reason for his feelings, he turned to the pile of envelopes and notebook pages before him.

Two hours later Tanner wished he'd let Stuart handle this.

Torn between exasperation and amusement, he still wasn't sure he'd gotten through to her. Her rationale in her creative bookkeeping could drive a saint into a tailspin, much less a hardheaded, bottom-line-oriented businessman.

"That's it. If you follow those suggestions, I guarantee you'll show a jump in your profit the first month," he said, leaning back and stretching.

Lowering his arms, he caught her looking quickly away. Had she been watching him? A gratified satisfaction swept through him. He'd looked at her enough. Good to know the shoe was on the other foot once in a while.

"I don't know. To demand so much money up front seems to make the whole business so mercenary, somehow."

"Mercenary? Sunny, you're in business to make money, right?"

"I guess."

"You guess? You have to know that much. If this is just a hobby—"

"No, I want to support myself. Just not make a lot of money."

"Why not?"

"Why?"

"Why what?"

Was he losing the trend of the conversation?

"Why should I want to make a lot of money? As long as I make enough to live on and to pay Eve, that's fine."

"Your business has to make money to keep you and Eve employed. And why not make all you can?"

"Lots of money is nice, but not necessary to enjoy life."

"It sure is."

He knew that for a fact. Money made a world of difference, from how well a person lived, to the opinion of others.

"So tell me, Mr. Rich Man, how do you enjoy your money? What do you do with your leisure time that uses lots of money? From the little I know about you, you don't even go home from the office at a reasonable time. You volunteer at that boys' club, which isn't exactly leisure activity, it must be a lot of work. I know you have season tickets to the symphony, but how often do you go? What do you spend your pots of money on?"

He reached for the empty coffee cup, looking into it as if it would miraculously give him some answer. When she laid it out like that, he had a hard time coming up with a satisfactory answer. He didn't do much more than work.

But he enjoyed that.

"Work gives me a feeling of satisfaction," he said slowly, meeting her gaze. "It's my hobby as well as my career."

"I like my job, too. I don't need lots of money to enjoy what I'm doing. I just do it. When a bride falls in love with one of my dresses, it sends me over the moon."

"One difference between us is that I am not in danger of losing my business because I enjoy my work."

"No, you're too ruthless to let that happen."

"I'm not running a charity."

"I don't want charity."

"Then stop running your business like one. It's not unreasonable for you to demand one-third of the cost of the gown at the commissioning, one-third at the first fitting and the balance at the final fitting. That way, you wouldn't have taken such a loss on that dress on the mannequin."

"How do you know about that dress?"

"Eve told me."

She looked away, clearly unhappy with his directive.

"Someone will buy it. It's such a beautiful dress. I love it. It was one of my better creations," she said slowly, defensively.

"It is pretty, no one's denying that. All I'm saying is you wouldn't have taken such a loss if the woman had paid for two-thirds before she decided to cancel."

"I guess."

"And you'll start buying in quantity?"

"When I can afford it," she nodded. "I know that makes good sense, but right now money is a bit tight. As you well know."

"I can lend you what you need. It's foolish to keep buying one item at a time when even a small multiple order can save you over twenty percent."

"I don't want to borrow any more money," she said stiffly, her eyes flashing when she faced him. "That's what got me in this mess in the first place."

"We're not talking a lot of money, not compared to what you already owe. Look on it as protecting my investment. If you find me a wife, I erase the debt."

"And if you don't like anyone I introduce?"

"Then Brides and Bows will be in a better financial state when I take it over."

She balled her fists and leaned closer.

Tanner felt his heart kick into higher gear and the delight he always felt around her rev up. Now what?

"You can't have my shop. If I have to introduce you to every single woman in San Francisco I will do so. But you have to do your part and make some sort of effort. I can't do it all myself."

"You're pretty when you're angry," he said.

"What?"

Her eyes widened and she sat back in her chair as if stunned.

Tanner smiled. For once he'd thrown her off balance. Maybe that was the key, say outrageous things when she least expected it. She did it enough around him, he should take a page out of her book.

"You heard me. In fact, Sunny, I'm surprised you're not married already. When I first met you, I thought Sean had set me up—you know, trying a bit of match-making between us."

"Us? As in you and me? Not in this lifetime."

"Ouch, and why not?"

"For one thing, I'm not sleek and sophisticated, in case you hadn't noticed," she said, tilting her head. "My mother's family goes back for generations, but my father's —my real father's family—doesn't. He was just a cop. Killed in the line of duty. And I don't have money of my own. Wouldn't you be worried I'd be marrying you for your money?"

He laughed, tilted back on the two back legs of the chair and tucked his fingers into his pockets.

"No, especially after your enlightening discussion of earlier. Money's not a primary issue with you. Love is."

"Darn straight. When I marry, I want a husband who loves me. Who wants to spend time with me, not hang around work until all hours making money. I want someone who takes an interest in my business, who will help me cook dinner and do his bit around the house. We'd do things together, like go on hikes, or down to the beach. Or just ride the cable cars and people watch."

"You don't have expensive tastes," he murmured, intrigued to find out what she thought of as an ideal marriage.

"Well, I wouldn't mind going on a cruise," she said slowly, watching him carefully.

"A cruise?"

"Mom and Theo went on one a couple of years ago and loved it. I've wished ever since that I could take one."

"Lying in the sun, having someone wait on you hand and foot?"

"Actually it was an Alaskan cruise and I was thinking more about all the food I could eat."

"Especially the shrimp and chocolate?"

She smiled and Tanner knew then he wanted to kiss her again. More than when he'd first arrived. More than during the evening when her fingers would brush against his, or when her unique special scent invaded his nostrils.

Her smile lightened everything, and he wanted to capture some of that light for himself.

Without thinking things through, he reached out and pulled her from her chair into his lap.

"What—"

His mouth cut off the rest of the sentence. For a long moment Sunny held still, then she relaxed and leaned into him, her arms encircling his neck as she pressed again his chest.

Capturing light and sunshine wasn't easy. But her kiss buoyed his spirits. He truly liked Sunny Pritchard. He'd miss her when he married and couldn't spend the evenings with her. Pulling back, he gazed down at her flushed face, her eyes drowsy and soft, her cheeks fused with color, her lips slightly swollen from the pressure of his.

She looked adorable.

For a moment he wondered if his plan was sound. Maybe he should consider Sunny as his choice.

No—bad idea.

She wanted more than he had in him to give. Love, and sharing, and devotion. He wanted a wife who would grace his table, be an asset in business, bring impeccable breeding to their children. He wanted entrée into the finest homes in the city and needed a wife who could provide that. Being allied with a powerful family would go far to cement his place in San Francisco society and business community.

The specter of his childhood would be banished forever.

"I have to go."

He stood, easing Sunny to her feet.

"Sure. Thanks for the lecture on accounting," she said, clearly confused by his abrupt departure.

"Any time. Follow some of the things I outlined, it will make it a lot easier to keep track of your exact situation."

"Right, and insist I get paid up front."

"At least enough to cover your expenses if someone decides to cancel at the last minute."

"It was one dress. I won't have any trouble finding someone to love it as much as I do."

"Right."

He headed for the door, needing to get some air. He didn't like the feelings that seemed to grow each time he was around

Sunny.

Jealousy about her seeing Joseph Thurmond Sanger the Fourth. Desire that grew each day.

And the uncertainty that was beginning to blossom about his original goal.

He knew better than to get sidetracked once he established his objective. Time to get on track again and get this over with.

"Are we still on for Saturday?" she asked at the door.

He took a breath, and nodded. One day, what could it hurt? And they wouldn't be locked up in her cozy, homey apartment, just the two of them. They'd be outside, surrounded by strangers.

"I'll pick you up around nine."

"See you then, Tanner," she said softly, her eyes holding a mysterious message deep in their depths.

San Francisco's famous fog covered the city Saturday morning, cool and damp. The day hadn't started auspiciously. Tanner wondered what Sunny would want to do in such weather. Nothing appealed much to him.

A walk on the beach was out. It was too cold and damp. People watching was probably out, as well, who else would be wandering around in this pea soup? Even riding his motorcycle was out. Too cold for that.

He parked his car two blocks from her apartment, finding no place closer. Knowing his mood wasn't the sunniest, he stood before her door and wondered if he should just cancel the entire day. It opened before he decided.

"I didn't ring," he said, taking in the bright picture she made. Jeans faded so much from washing they were almost white, but not quite. A pale blue sweater over a dark blue shirt. Her blond hair curled every which way—probably due to the dampness in the air.

"You didn't have to ring. It is precisely nine, and you're always on time."

She grinned in triumph and tilted her head.

"Want to come in or are we ready to go?"

"Where do you want to go? In case you haven't looked outside, it's miserable."

"Not so, just refreshing and exciting, like San Francisco. We have the gift of a cool day to do whatever we want. Eve's covering the shop, so I'm footloose and fancy free. What's first?"

He scowled at her. Perky had its place. Today was not it.

"I'd planned to take you on a bay cruise. Not quite like the ocean liners, but a cruise," he said slowly.

"I've never been. That's great."

"We'd see nothing, this fog is right down to the ground."

"It'll burn off by afternoon. Let's do something else this morning and then we can do the cruise thing. I'm ready."

"Grab a jacket, it's cold outside."

In two minutes they were on the sidewalk in front of her house.

"No bike?" she asked, looking around.

"Too cold and damp. I brought my car, but couldn't find a place to park on your street. It's not far."

"I don't mind walking, I like it. Do you ever just walk around the city?"

"Not in recent memory," he murmured, remembering days when walking was his only mode of transportation.

Sunny laughed. "No, I suppose you are too busy to walk around. You probably take a cab or drive yourself anywhere you want to go."

"Pretty much."

"Well, I don't want to just drive in the fog. What did you have planned?"

Tanner paused. He'd planned on the cruise. Then maybe lunch somewhere and let the afternoon take care of itself.

"Earth to Tanner," Sunny said, touching his hand.

His fingers curled around hers and he looked down at her.

"I'm more used to quiet dinners and nightclubs," he said.

"Don't you date on the weekends?" she asked.

"I rarely date at all."

"Of course, too busy playing workaholic. Time you had a bit of fun. Especially before marrying your trophy bride and having your two point six children. Shall I make a couple of suggestions?"

"No, I think I can handle things."

They reached his car and he unlocked the door.

"A Mercedes, now why am I not surprised?" Sunny murmured as she slid into the leather seat.

"Probably because you wouldn't admit to surprise even if you were," he retorted as he sat behind the wheel.

"Powerful, stylish, and expensive, the perfect car for the rising executive."

"I've risen, in case you hadn't noticed."

"On the backs of little people like me."

"Hey, babe, if you want to play with the big boys, you need to toughen up."

"Ha! Stay out of shark-infested waters, you mean."

"Did you sign that loan document with your eyes open?" he asked as he pulled into traffic.

"Yes, but I was dealing with Brad Peterson, and he didn't seem nearly as ruthless as you."

Tanner kept quiet. He didn't like the fact she considered him ruthless. Hadn't he agreed to forgive the debt if she came up with a suitable candidate?

"Where are we going?" Sunny asked after a moment of silence.

"Union Square," he said.

"Why?"

"You'll see."

"Tell me about some of your other friends," she said, settling back in the seat and gazing out the window.

"Which friends?" he asked.

"Well, not me or Sean. Others."

She waved her hand.

"Most of my friends, as you call them, are really business acquaintances. Except for Phil."

"Who's Phil?"

"Director at the boys' center."

Sunny looked at him closely.

"I was teasing when I said you work all the time, but maybe I was closer to the truth than I expected. Do you ever do things for fun, just pure plain fun? Or is everything directed toward building a fortune? I know you had a tough childhood, but don't let that rob you of what you can enjoy now. You've made a bundle, cut loose and enjoy some of it."

"I'm hoping we'll enjoy today," he said stiffly.

His life suited him or had until Sean had thrown him at Sunny. Maybe it was a mistake.

If he hadn't attended that charity ball with Marie, he and Sean wouldn't have run into each other. No, it was more if he'd kept quiet about his quest, this wouldn't be happening.

Glancing at Sunny, he smiled slowly. But he'd miss today with his new friend. All the aggravation she threw at him was worth today.

"Are we going to ride a cable car?" Sunny asked after he parked the car at Union Square and headed for Powell and Market. They joined the queue waiting for the next cable car near Union Square.

"And why not?"

"I can't picture it, that's all."

"What's to picture? We get on, sit down, buy a ticket, get off when we reach Chinatown."

"We're going to Chinatown?"

Her eyes lit up and she smiled broadly.

"That's great."

"I remember you saying you'd like to explore every shop in Chinatown," he said as the line moved forward.

When a tourist loaded with cameras blundered into Sunny, Tanner pulled her closer, turning a bit to shelter her from the pedestrians on the sidewalk. His arm around her shoulder felt good. She snuggled right up against him as if she belonged.

"That's sweet, that you remembered what I said and planned for us to spend part of the day there."

He nodded, pleased he'd remembered that at the last second. At least prowling the shops in Chinatown would be warm, she wouldn't be out in the damp.

"And we can eat dim sum for lunch."

"What?" he asked.

"Dim sum. You do like dim sum, don't you?"

"Chinese food?"

"Lunch, you know where they push the cart around and you pick and choose what you want to eat."

Sunny pulled back enough to see his face.

"Sounds fine."

"You've never eaten dim sum, have you? I can't believe it, born and raised right here in San Francisco and never eaten dim sum? Have you eaten on North Beach? Or do you limit your restaurants to those that populate the financial district?"

"I've eaten at some of the best Italian restaurants on North Beach. And at the wharf, and the top of the Mark. I don't limit myself to the financial district. I just haven't eaten dim sum."

"It is lunch, you probably can't tear yourself away from work."

He lifted her chin with a finger and caught her gaze.

"No more slanderous comments about my work. We're out here to have fun and I don't appreciate your deprecating my career."

She blinked.

"I'm sorry. You're right."

Before she could say any more, their cable car arrived. They watched the brakeman and conductor push the car on the turnstile until it faced up Powell Street. Joining the surge of people, they scrambled for an outside seat. Sunny squeezed in against Tanner and turned her shining face to his.

"This is so much fun. It's been ages since I've ridden one."

"Good," he returned.

An unusual feeling settled around his heart. Refusing to give it a name, Tanner watched her as the cable car lurched and started up the hill, fascinated anew at her enthusiasm over the most commonplace things.

It was a day out of time, Tanner thought as he and Sunny wandered in and out of the numerous shops lining Grant Avenue. Neither spoke about the past, nor their respective businesses, nor of anything earth-shattering. But every moment was priceless.

He loved watching her examine the lace or the carved wooden scenes, then put them down with a gentle smile at the proprietor.

"Want to buy one?" he asked as they regained the sidewalk after one episode.

"Good heavens, no, where would I put it? But they're so intricately carved, I'm fascinated. And the lace is lovely. I might want some for a gown or veil."

"If you don't plan to buy anything, why are we shopping?" he asked.

"We're shopping, not buying. Looking, browsing. Don't you enjoy looking at things, try to figure out how they were made?"

"Not particularly."

"Well, I do. Come on, I want to stop in this one."

Sunny took his hand and Tanner threaded his fingers through hers. He didn't care if they went into a hundred shops—she was pleased with the day and he wanted her to enjoy it.

Did she do this kind of thing with Joseph Thurmond Sanger?

They stopped for dim sum at a restaurant a block up from Grant Avenue. Crowded with families and couples, it bustled with energy. They were lucky to get a table almost immediately. Sunny ordered jasmine tea and looked at the first cart that passed their table.

"Shall I order things for us?" she asked.

Tanner nodded.

"Do you know what everything is?"

"Not a clue, just what's good and what I want to avoid. This is pork."

She pointed to a steamed dumpling.

"They have lots of shrimp items."

"Now I know why you like dim sum."

She laughed. "Maybe you're right. This is so much fun. Thanks for asking me out today," she said.

"I'm glad you're enjoying yourself. Do they have forks at this place?" he asked, picking up the chopsticks.

"I doubt it. We can ask or you can learn to use chopsticks. I'll show you."

By the time Tanner managed to competently transfer food from his plate to his mouth with chopsticks, he felt he could handle anything. It was tedious and treacherous, but he was determined to master the art that Sunny made seem so effortless.

Her laughter and joy at his efforts had nothing to do with his perseverance.

"At the risk of sounding like your mother, learning new things is good for you," she said.

He shrugged.

"I don't know what my mother would have said. She left long before I could remember her."

The smile faded from her face.

"I'm sorry. I didn't know."

He caught her eye and smiled.

"No problem, she left when I was small. She didn't like living in the Tenderloin, I guess."

"And your father never remarried?"

" No. "

Eating the last bite from her plate she laid down the chopsticks and took a sip of the hot tea.

"So founding your own family is very important, isn't it?"

"Yes. And it has to be the right family. I don't want any child of mine to ever question anything. I want him to know his grandparents, to know his place in life. And not to have to..."

"To what?" she said when he fell silent.

"Nothing. If you're finished, want to head for the wharf? If the fog's lifted a bit, we can still get on that cruise."

"I hope you get the perfect wife, Tanner," she said gently.

"If not, it won't be for lack of trying, now will it?" he asked.

7

It was after dark by the time Tanner brought Sunny home. The bay cruise had been a success, despite the cold wind and the fog that still hovered.

When they'd returned to the Embarcadero, Sunny discovered Tanner had never been to Pier 39 and insisted they make that their next stop. She cajoled him in to buying truffles at the chocolate shop, browsed through the specialty shops that catered to tourists by carrying every imaginable trinket emblazoned with the words San Francisco.

They ate at a small restaurant specializing in clam chowder and sourdough bread.

He had laughed, and argued, and felt more alive than any time in the last few years. No wonder Joseph Thurmond Sanger wanted to spend time with her, Sunny was a delight.

The cable car ride from the wharf back to Union Square sped by. Because night had fallen, lights sparkled from the buildings, muted by the defusing aspect of the thick fog.

"I hope you had as much fun today as I did," Sunny said when he pulled into a tight parking space only two buildings from her apartment.

"I'm glad you enjoyed yourself," he said. "I'll walk you up."

Tanner wanted to be invited in for coffee. He didn't want the day to end.

"No need to do that, I can manage," she said quickly.

"I want to."

"Oh."

Sunny was unusually silent on the short walk to her apartment. She said nothing as Tanner took the keys from her hand and unlocked her door, opening it and waiting for her to proceed him into the dark apartment. His fist closed over her keys. He'd give them back once he was inside.

"Would you like coffee, or something?" she asked, diffidently pausing.

"Yes."

He stepped inside and closed the door behind him. Opening his palm, he offered her keys. The brush of her fingertips against his skin strengthened the shimmering attraction that hovered all day.

Without a word, he pulled her into his arms and kissed her. She pushed against him after a moment and broke free.

"I don't think we should be doing that," she said, her eyes lowered.

"Why not?" he asked.

He'd kissed her before. She'd never protested.

Turning, almost running, Sunny headed for the kitchen.

"I'll fix some coffee and we can talk for a bit. Then you'll have to leave. I have to get up early tomorrow—"

She stopped suddenly as if she'd run out of words.

"Why do you have to get up early on a Sunday?" he asked, following her.

What was wrong? She'd changed in the few moments from the car to her apartment. They'd spent a pleasant day together. Suddenly it was as if she couldn't stand to be near him.

"I just do, all right? Do you want cream in your coffee?"

"No, I drink it black."

He was disappointed she hadn't remembered. Which was stupid. Just because he remembered she liked hers laced liberally with cream didn't mean she had to pay attention to his likes or dislikes.

Leaning casually against the counter, his arms crossed over his chest, he watched her start the coffee machine, take cups down from the cupboard and rummage in the refrigerator for cream. She turned on the water, let it run hot, and dampened a dishrag, wiping the immaculate counters.

"Something bothering you, Sunny?" he asked.

Tension stretched between them, rising every moment. There was definitely something wrong, but he couldn't figure out what it was.

"No. Coffee will be ready in a minute, why don't you go sit in the living room?"

"I don't mind waiting here," he said easily, his eyes never leaving her.

"I do, you make me nervous."

Tanner raised his eyebrows in surprise to hear anything made her nervous.

"I make you nervous?"

She nodded and swallowed hard, licking her lips and looking thoroughly exasperated. Instantly Tanner wanted to feel that moisture on her lips with his, kiss her throat, feel that pulse point beat against his lips.

"You keep staring at me," she snapped, glaring at him.

He smiled and nodded.

"You're easy on the eyes."

"Well, take your eyes and go in the living room. I'll bring the coffee out when it's done."

Tanner shrugged and pushed away from the counter. Her behavior baffled him, but he hadn't come inside to make her angry. If she wanted a few minutes to herself, he'd give it to her.

He glanced out her window, but the swirling fog hid any view she might claim. Taking a seat on the comfortable sofa, he leaned back on the cushions, stretching his legs out. The room was fussy for his tastes, but reflected the romanticism that comprised much of Sunny's makeup. It was growing on him.

Five minutes later she joined him, a mug of coffee in each hand. Carefully placing them on the low table before the sofa, she chose the nearby chair, rather than join Tanner on the sofa.

"You wanted to talk?"

He didn't want to talk. He wanted her to sit beside him, where he could feel her presence, be enticed by her scent, touch her, kiss her.

"I thought I'd give you a thumbnail sketch of the women I think will be at the party next Saturday. You can decide ahead of time which ones you might like to meet so we don't miss anyone who would be a qualified candidate."

"I think I need to meet them all."

Sunny sighed and reached for her coffee cup.

"The thing is, Tanner, sometimes I don't think you're putting forth the effort you need in order to find a wife. I can only do so much. You should have taken Julie or Carmella out today. You're wasting time with me. I'm not your type."

"I enjoyed the day. And probably for the very reason that there is nothing between us except a business deal. Think how awkward it would be if you were interested in me from a romantic point."

"Right."

She blew on her coffee and took a sip, her eyes on the cup.

"Enjoy it while you can," she muttered. "The clock strikes midnight and it all ends."

"What do you mean?"

She glanced up, looked away.

"Nothing much. Think about it for a minute. It was obvious today that you don't often spend your Saturdays as we did. And probably won't after you marry your paragon."

"You don't think my future wife can enjoy the kind of day we just spent?"

"I have trouble picturing Carmella wanting to take a bay cruise in the fog. Or anytime, for that matter. And I doubt she'd ride a cable car unless every cab in the city was on strike."

"Carmella is out of the running, I told you that."

He didn't like the trend of the conversation. Time enough later to talk about a future wife. He wanted to enjoy the rest of the evening with Sunny. Her perspective on things was refreshing, a bit wacky sometimes, but always kind and optimistic. He liked her enthusiasm for the ordinary and her genuine interest in living for the moment.

"My point is, that if you want sophisticated and elegant, you're not going to get rowdy and adventuresome. The two don't mesh. Not that I would presume to tell you what kind of wife you need. You seem very certain of what you want."

"I am," he said firmly.

He'd thought about it for years. He knew exactly the kind of woman he wanted for his wife, for the mother of his son. He had enough money to attract anyone he wanted.

For a moment he looked at Sunny. She'd be disappointed in his thoughts. She believed so much in love and wanted it for everyone.

"Your father and mother loved each other, I presume," he said.

"Passionately."

She smiled, lost in memories for a moment.

"I was too young then to really realize how special that love was. But they were forever kissing and touching and caressing each other and me. Hugs were plentiful, kisses abundant. And I still remember the dazed disbelief with which my mother lived for years after he died. It was as if a part of herself was gone forever."

"But she remarried."

"About five years later. Theo had known her for a long time, but it was as if she couldn't see any man for years. Then she began to date again. Theo was number three, I think. And the last man she went out with. He wooed her in every way imaginable."

"And had the money to afford extravagant gestures, I bet."

Sunny flared up at that.

"Take that back. It wasn't anything like that. He loves her and did everything he could to show her that, but he didn't need to spend a lot of money to do it. And Mom wouldn't have been impressed with money. She came from money. But she and Daddy didn't have much. The love they shared was so strong, they didn't miss having tons of money. Theo was smart enough to realize that and did not flaunt his wealth. If anything, it would have turned Mom off."

Tanner held out a hand, palm out. She looked like a kitten, ruffled fur and hissing.

"Back off, wildcat. My mistake. I knew your mother refused to move home after your father died. My mistake thinking she'd like an easier life with Theo than struggling to make ends meet on her own."

"Shows what you know, Mr. Rich Man."

"Change of subject. I've engaged a limousine for Saturday. Where is this party? I need to let the driver know."

"A limo? Why can't you drive? Or I can if you like. It's just to Toddy and Denise's. They live in Westborough. Jeez, Tanner, we don't need a limo."

"Indulge me, sweets. I might care to have a drink or two at the party and don't want to drink and drive."

"And you can afford it," she said waspishly.

"I prefer to look on it as putting a bit of money back into the economy."

Sunny laughed aloud.

"I can't believe you said that. You no more think about putting money into the economy than... than you believe in love."

Since his diversion succeeded in drawing a response that was spontaneous and sincere, he decided to leave before she got herself worked up over something unimportant again.

"Thanks for the coffee. I'll pick you up next Saturday at seven-thirty."

She blinked.

"You're leaving already. You haven't finished your coffee."

"It's time to go."

He rose and waited for her to stand up.

"Thank you for a great day, Tanner. I had fun."

"I did, too."

He walked to the door. Leaning over, he skimmed his lips over hers. He didn't hold her or press his luck.

She'd already rejected him once tonight, he didn't want a second time.

"Tanner."

She reached out and touched his arm.

"Money's only important when you don't have it. You're not that poor kid living in the Tenderloin now. You have enough money that if you stopped work tomorrow, you'd never want for anything again. There's more to life than acquiring money and spending it. Let yourself discover the other joys out there."

"Philosophy at ten o'clock?" he asked dryly.

She nodded, her eyes serious and sincere.

"Find your perfect wife, but make sure you like her and can enjoy life with her. Marriage is for such a long time."

"I know what I want, Sunny. And when I get it, I'll hold on to it."

Twice during the week Tanner almost called Sunny. Each time he hesitated. Her manner when they reached her apartment disturbed him. She'd seemed different, remote almost. He knew he'd pushed for their date, but she'd enjoyed herself, he knew it. She was too transparent to dissemble about that.

He wondered if she were seeing Joseph Thurmond Sanger this week. Would it be better to know one way or the other or better to remain ignorant? He didn't like her dating Joe, but he had no hold over her. She was free to see whomever she wished.

Each time he reached for the phone, he changed his mind. He'd wait until Saturday.

Promptly at seven-thirty Saturday evening Tanner rang the doorbell to Sunny's apartment. When she opened the door, he was stunned.

"Come in. I still have to get my shoes," she said, her eyes sparkling.

But the sparkle in her eyes barely outshone the sparkle in the diamonds that she wore.

Tanner stepped inside and stared at her. Twirling his index finger, he motioned her to turn around. The dark blue dress appeared to have been designed expressly for her. It fit like a second skin, displaying every taut curve, every sleek line. Ending above her knees, it displayed her shapely black nylon-clad legs to full advantage. The thin straps and low neckline perfectly framed the bib of diamonds that hung around her throat. Diamond ear studs caught the light and drew the eye to the sleek hairstyle that looked as unlike Sunny as everything he'd just seen.

Dramatic and sophisticated, it changed her entirely.

The makeup emphasized her eyes and the perfection of her lips.

Sleek and sophisticated were excellent choices of words to describe the vision before him.

"Sunny?"

"What?"

Those dramatic eyes narrowed as she stared at him.

"Just checking to make sure it was the right woman. You look fantastic."

She grinned and he recognized the lopsided smile.

"I clean up real good, wouldn't you say? Have to hold my own at these kinds of events. I'll see everyone in my age group at this party. And most of them use any excuse to try for one-upmanship. I've often thought a really smart thief would hit up one of these and take all the jewelry we're wearing. He could retire for life after such a heist. I'll get my shoes, I'll just be a sec."

He watched her hurry to her bedroom, entranced with the sway of her hips, the sassy flash of legs as she moved soundlessly down the hall. For a moment he hesitated, unsure he wanted to go to the party. He'd rather stay home and discover more about Sunny.

The last thing he'd expected tonight was to find her dressed like a fashion model and carrying off the sophistication he'd glimpsed in Marie and Carmella.

Yet why not? She'd grown up with Marie, Carmella and Julie. She'd gone to the right schools, came from old money and had a mother who probably taught her everything she needed to know to hold her own in San Francisco society.

How many other facets were there to this woman?

When she left her bedroom, she wore strappy high heels and carried an evening wrap. Detouring through the living room, she scooped up a fancy wrapped present, and hurried to join Tanner.

"Should I have bought a gift?" he asked, spying the package she carried.

"Nope. You don't even know them yet. But I've been friends with Denise for years."

"Didn't you say you hadn't planned to attend, until you decided it would be the perfect place for me to meet your friends?"

She nodded.

He indicated the dress and diamonds.

"Last-minute choice? No worrying about nothing to wear?"

"Yes, well it is a bit much, sometimes."

She ran her hand down over her hips, and Tanner followed, wishing it was his hand following the soft flare of hip.

"This is not really me. I prefer wearing jeans like last weekend. And there'll be so many people there, I won't really get to visit much with Toddy and Denise, so it seemed like a waste of time. But now we have another goal."

"Toddy, is that a nickname?"

Tanner reached out to draw her wrap from her arms and hold it for her to put on.

"His actual name is William. But in college he fell prey to hot toddies. He loved them and usually ended up drunk as a skunk. So the nickname stuck. He doesn't imbibe quite so freely now that he's gained a bit of wisdom. But if you ever want to bribe him, do it with a hot toddy."

"I doubt I need to bribe anyone," Tanner murmured, drawing in a deep breath.

The soft fragrance that was pure Sunny delighted him.

He'd missed it this past week. He'd missed her.

"Well, let's get this show on the road. And, Tanner..."

She caught his arm and looked into his eyes.

"This is it. You will find someone tonight or all bets are off. And I have fulfilled my part of this crazy deal you and Sean concocted. You have to go into this with an open mind. Do you hear?"

He smiled, amused by her lecture.

"I hear. I'll let you know later if the deal has been fulfilled."

Anger flashed in her eyes, but he didn't care. Leaning closer he kissed her. The taste of lip gloss different from that of her natural lips. Beneath it, he could feel her warmth.

"We'll talk later," he promised. "Come, my lady, your coach awaits. Did I tell you how beautiful you look tonight?"

She shook her head and slowly allowed a small smile.

"Sleek and sophisticated?" she asked slyly.

"Definitely. Maybe I should be looking a bit closer to home for a bride?"

Her smile saddened.

"No, Tanner. We wouldn't suit. The things we each want are too different."

She was right, of course. But for a moment he let the fantasy invade his mind. Marrying Sunny, living with her in his apartment overlooking the marina. They'd each go to work in the morning, meet for lunch a couple of times a week, cook dinner together. And the weekends, the ones he didn't spend at the boys' club, would be spent together, doing things together.

He wouldn't be alone anymore.

He wouldn't be consumed with work.

He'd have Sunny.

Lights blazed from every window in the large house the limo stopped in front of. The sound of laughter, conversation and soft music wafted from the windows, left open to cool down the rooms.

The driver opened the back door and Tanner assisted Sunny from the vehicle, glad he'd hired the limo. There wasn't a parking place in sight.

Sunny handed the gift and her wrap to the maid who opened the door. Glancing at Tanner, her eyes widened.

"Oops."

She brushed his lips with her thumb, then a second time.

"Lipstick," she muttered, looking at the red stain on her thumb.

He chuckled and drew out his handkerchief. Running it over his mouth once to make sure she'd gotten all traces, he took her hand and began to wipe the smear from her thumb.

"Hazards of kissing a beautiful woman dressed to the nines," he murmured.

"Do I need to replenish it?" she asked, tilting her head up for his perusal.

"Not unless I kiss you again."

She backed away.

"Not here."

"I'm not exactly an ogre."

Anger touched him at her retreat.

"Of course not, you idiot. But you're here looking for someone else. If people see you kissing me they're going to get entirely the wrong impression."

"I'm not sure I care."

"Sunny, how nice to see you."

A tall red-haired woman sailed into the foyer.

"I thought I heard the bell a minute ago. How have you been?"

She touched her cheek to Sunny's and smiled in welcome.

"Hi, Denise. I've been great. You look wonderful. Happy anniversary. Marriage obviously agrees with you."

"Oh, honey, it's more than that. Toddy and I are expecting."

"Wow, I can't believe it. You two are going to be parents?"

"Yes, but not for about six more months. In the meantime, I don't believe I know your date."

Denise linked arms with Sunny and smiled brightly at Tanner.

"Oh, sorry. Tanner, I'd like you to meet Denise. Denise, this is Tanner Wright."

"How nice to meet you, Tanner. I've heard a lot about you, mostly from the papers. Sean's here and he said he thought you'd be coming with Sunny. Come on in and mingle. We've got to get together soon, Sunny."

"Absolutely, Denise. I want to hear all about the blessed event."

The large living room was crowded with men and women talking, laughing and moving from group to group. Few people used the furniture, most were standing. Sunny hesitated in the archway.

"Do you want to get a drink or something before we begin to mingle?" she asked Tanner.

At his nod, she led the way to the dining room where the long table had been pushed to one wall and was laden with canapés. By the door to the kitchen a bar had been set up. They ordered drinks from the bartender.

"Hi, Sunny. I didn't know you were coming."

A tall, thin young man bent to kiss her cheek.

She smiled at him.

"Hi, Joe. I didn't plan to come originally, but then decided I needed to toast the happy couple."

When the man looked at Tanner, Sunny rushed into speech. "Tanner, this is Joe. Joe, Tanner."

Joe nodded his head once. "Tanner."

Suspecting who the man was, Tanner stepped closer to Sunny and placed his hand on her shoulder. Her bare shoulder. Slipping his fingers beneath the thin straps that held her dress, he pulled her closer.

"Joe as in Joseph Thurmond Sanger the Fourth?" he asked, his narrowed gaze assessing the man before him.

In other circumstances, he might have liked him. Joe carried himself confidently without an arrogant swagger. Apparently completely at ease in the surroundings. Of course, he'd been born to this life.

Tanner resented him instantly.

Joe laughed and looked at Sunny, his eyes lingering on the possessive hold Tanner had made.

"You didn't tell him that, did you?" he asked Sunny.

Color rose in her cheeks and she looked confused.

"I think I did ages ago. Why not, it's your name."

"Come on, Sunny—Joseph Thurmond Sanger the Fourth? I don't go around telling friends you are Sunshine Elizabeth Pritchard the First."

Before she could reply, Tanner tightened his grip. Joe knew her middle name, he hadn't. He didn't like the implied intimacy between the two.

"Excuse us, Joe? Sunny's promised to introduce me to someone."

"Sure. Nice to meet you."

Tanner couldn't parrot the words. He nodded and moved from the large room, dodging another couple, sheltering Sunny from bumping into them.

"I can't believe that."

She took a sip of her drink and stopped dead.

"I just can't believe you did that. Get your hand off me."

"Don't cause a scene," he said, moving his hand, reluctant to release that tantalizing soft skin.

"Don't cause a scene? You haven't seen anything if you think my calmly asking you to remove your hand is a scene. But if you want one, I'm just the person to cause it."

"I don't want one. What's wrong? I just put my hand on your shoulder."

"Listen, I've been around men long enough to recognize a possessive move. You almost stood on a table and told Joe hands off. I can't believe you did that."

She looked at him suspiciously.

"You acted almost jealous," she accused.

"In case you forgot, we're here tonight for you to introduce me to eligible candidates for my wife, not to meet all your boyfriends."

"All my—one man. And he's not a boyfriend. He's a friend."

"Tanner? This is getting to be a habit, man."

Sean stopped and held out his hand.

"Whoa, did you bring Sunny?" he asked as the men shook hands.

"She brought me," Tanner replied.

"Much to my regret, I might add," she said, seething.

"You're here now, Sean, you take him under control. I have to go to the ladies."

Tanner reached out and caught her arm.

"Truly?"

"Truly," she said sweetly. "Otherwise I'm tempted to throw this glass of wine over your head."

She pulled away and stormed across the room.

"Trouble in paradise?" Sean asked, watching his cousin.

"Nothing I can't handle," Tanner replied.

He watched as she rounded a corner and was lost from sight.

"Right. You can handle anything. So how do you like Sunny?"

"She's enough to drive a man crazy."

"Yes. But isn't she a love?"

Tanner closed his eyes briefly at the word. Opening them, he looked at Sean.

"She brought me tonight to meet some of her friends."

"I thought you two were a duo," Sean said, puzzled.

"I can't imagine why. She's not what I'm looking for in a wife," Tanner replied blandly.

Bridling, Sean's gaze hardened.

"Why not?"

"Back off, Sean. Sunny and I wouldn't suit. I'm looking for a bit more sophistication—"

"Did you see her tonight? She's as sophisticated as they get."

"She's looking for love and I don't even believe in it," Tanner said.

"Not believe in it, or just never experienced it?" Sean asked shrewdly.

"Neither. My parents said they loved each other and look at the mess they made of their lives. My father said he loved me and neglected me completely, did not care for anyone or anything but liquor. Love is an illusion and one I plan to do without."

"I loved Betsy. I still miss her, every day."

"She died twelve years ago, Sean, past time to move on."

"Right. I could be a workaholic like you. Sunny's a saint to put up with you. I'm sorry now that I suggested the plan. I hope you find someone tonight so she's out of it."

Sean spun around and headed for the bar. He never looked back.

"Blast it," Tanner said softly.

"Tanner?" Carmella Randolph stopped and smiled at him. "Nice to see you again. I didn't know you were a friend of Toddy's."

"I came with Sunny. In fact I have yet to meet the host, though Denise greeted us at the door," he said, already wishing Sunny had returned.

"Come on and I'll introduce you around. Where did Sunny go?"

By the time Tanner spotted Sunny sometime later, he'd met four young women all friends of Carmella's. Studying them casually, he found himself completely unmoved by any of them.

Keeping an eye open for Sunny, his mind had wandered. He knew she was mad at his behavior when meeting her friend Joe, but darn it, she'd made a bargain and he expected her to be making the introductions, and giving him background information on the people he met, not Carmella. Where was she?

Spying her near the door, Tanner left the group he'd been a part of and headed in Sunny's direction. She'd had enough time to sulk. "

Sunny, are you all right?" he asked when he drew close enough.

She nodded.

"Fine."

Taking a breath, she tossed her head and smiled. It didn't reach her eyes.

"Let's mingle, Tanner. That's our sole reason for being here, right?"

"Carmella's introduced me to a few people."

He didn't want to meet any more women. What he'd really like to do was take Sunny to the Crown Room and dance away the rest of the night. She looked so polished and lovely, he wanted to show her off to the world at the same time keep her for himself. Just the two of them.

"Who did you meet?"

"Christine Williams and her current date. Joyce Montgomery. Ellen Naylor."

"Ellen would be a good choice. Did you like her?"

He shrugged.

"She didn't brag about her father's wealth or talk my ear

off."

"Good start. Let's go find her and spend a bit more time with her."

Sunny led the way purposefully.

So much for his idea of dancing.

By the end of the evening Tanner's temper was frayed. He knew a wrong word would unleash his anger. Sunny had been the perfect matchmaker, drawing out Ellen and pointing out how much in common she and Tanner had.

At just the right moment, she'd excused herself and left the two of them near one of the windows. Tanner easily drew the young woman out further, but one part of him centered on Sunny.

He watched as she mingled with friends, kissed some, hugged some. Jealousy rose again. He wanted her attention on him. Wanted those kisses and hugs.

A discreet glance at his watch showed him it was almost time for the limo to arrive. Grateful he'd indicated a time to the driver, he explained to Ellen that he had to leave.

Fully aware she met many of the attributes he claimed he wanted in a wife, he asked if he could call her. She smiled and nodded, seeming pleased as she recited her phone number.

When he finished putting it in his phone, Tanner's gaze clashed with Sunny's. For a moment he couldn't read her expression, but just before she turned away, it looked shocked.

And sad.

8

Tanner sensed the tension in Sunny as they waited for the limousine. It swirled around them as the car drew up and they entered the luxury vehicle. When the door closed, enclosing them in the wide breadth of the car, Tanner turned to her.

"Is there a problem?" he asked, on the alert.

He knew something was wrong, but he was unable to pinpoint exactly what.

"Should there be? It seems as if we accomplished exactly what you wanted this evening. I introduced you to several eligible women whose families don't have a skeleton in the closet or a hidden agenda. You seemed especially chummy with Ellen Naylor. Is she the one, do you think? I'm sure she'll be a malleable wife. Just what you need to display the family jewels."

Her voice sounded distant, uninterested.

"Far too early to tell. I have her phone number. I thought I'd give her a call and invite her to dinner. I don't wish to chance lunch."

He hoped for a smile at that, but Sunny's lips were clamped in a distinctive line of disapproval.

After a moment she nodded.

"Sounds like a good plan."

"Any thoughts on how I should handle this?" Tanner asked a few moments later when Sunny remained silent.

She looked at him.

"I'm sure you can manage just fine. Be yourself, spend lots of money on her and she'll love you to death. Oh, no, not love. Well, she'll be glad to spend time with you. Help you decide how to spend all that money. You could have asked her when you two were being so chummy."

"We had other things to discuss."

Could it be she resented the time he spent with Ellen? Was Sunny jealous? What else could account for her cold voice, her snippy manner?

"I'm sure you did. And did she pass muster? Must have if you have invited her out. She's already ahead of Carmella and Julie."

"On the surface she seems to meet my requirements," he said calmly, intrigued by her behavior.

Not for the first time he wished he understood women better.

Sunny shook her head.

"Still sounds like you're getting a dog."

"I find her charming and likable. And she is easy on the eyes. Tell me some more about Ellen," he invited, interested to see if she thawed at all or stayed cool.

Was she jealous of his attention to Ellen? Did she want his attention focused on herself?

The car slid silently through the dark city streets, the motion soothing, in direct contrast to the tension that filled the interior. Had someone said something to upset Sunny, or was it more personal? For a moment he almost yielded to the urge to demand she tell him what the problem was so he could fix it.

"Ellen's family has been in California for generations. Her father inherited a lot of money and made even more in shipping. He branched into computers when Apple first started and increased the family wealth drastically. And they take care of their wealth. You'll have no worries about her marrying you for your money. She has more than she can spend in a lifetime. But I don't think she brags on her family's wealth like Carmella," Sunny said.

"And should I worry about any other aspect with Ellen?" he asked quickly.

She looked at him in confusion.

"I can't imagine what. She's been to the best schools, excels in small talk and probably will be totally intrigued with you. You've amassed a fortune, run a tremendously successful company, are welcomed everywhere, you two seem the perfect match with entree everywhere."

"Like your family welcomed me," he said softly.

"You're Sean's friend. I know Aunt Patty's fond of you as is Uncle Steve. Why wouldn't they welcome you? You're a bit dictatorial, but kind and generous with your time, look at your volunteer work. I don't know many men who give so much of themselves. Most just send money."

He shrugged.

"Anyway, I'm sure Ellen will be beside herself to be going out with you," she muttered, scooting farther away on the plush seat and staring out the tinted windows as the lights flashed by.

"At least our deal is complete."

"Not yet," he said, struck by the thought.

"Why not? I've fulfilled my part. I introduced you to half a dozen eligible women tonight. You liked Ellen, you said you're going to invite her out. What more do you want?"

"Some pointers on what she'd like, maybe."

He was clutching at straws, it sounded silly. But he didn't like Sunny's mentioning that their deal was ended. He wasn't ready to stop seeing Sunny.

"Take her to some fancy-do restaurant, order champagne, dance until the place closes. She'll love that. Make it very romantic. Women love that."

"Do you?"

"Do I what?"

Sunny looked at him warily.

"Like things romantic."

"We aren't discussing me. We're trying to finish this dumb deal. You like Ellen. Marry her and we're quits."

"Not quite. It's a bit early yet. Ellen and I may not suit."

"For goodness's sake, am I suppose to dangle until you finally tie the knot? Our agreement was to introduce you to eligible women. I've done it."

"It is finished when I say so. Since I hold the high cards, you don't have much to say in the matter."

She frowned and edged further away. If she moved any more, he thought, she'd be up against the door.

As the limo turned onto Chestnut Street, Tanner realized if he dated Ellen and liked her, he might well be on his way to marrying into an old San Francisco family.

The exultation he expected was missing.

Too early to feel triumph at achieving his goal. Time

enough for that if he decided Ellen was the one.

Glancing at Sunny, he realized if he and Ellen clicked that he would see Sunny occasionally as friends of both he and his wife. Somehow the thought disturbed.

"Do you need me to come to the boutique to help with your accounting?" he asked, wanting another tie to connect them.

He wasn't ready to give up his tentative friendship with this woman, not yet.

"I can manage. Just send the canceled note."

She waited in silence as the driver hurried to open her door.

"I'll call you after Ellen and I meet, in case I need further pointers."

He opened the back door and stepped to the curb, reaching out to assist Sunny.

"No need. Just send the canceled note. And I can get up to my apartment by myself."

She turned and almost ran up the three stone steps to the heavy front door. Tanner ignored her snappish behavior and accompanied her to her apartment. Reaching calmly for her keys, he was startled at how cold her fingers felt.

"Are you all right?" he asked.

"Fine. Goodbye, Tanner."

She snatched the keys from his fingers and hurried inside, closing the door in his face.

"Good night," he said, anger beginning to build.

He wasn't used to temperamental prima donnas. If that was how creative people reacted, he would do better to stick with businessmen.

"Blast it," Tanner swore Sunday afternoon.

All morning he'd been tempted to call Sunny to see if she wanted to spend the afternoon together. He'd spent the previous day at the boys' club working with the youngsters. The satisfaction he derived from sharing his time with those boys quietly filled a needed space within.

But the party they'd attended last night had fulfilled nothing. He didn't often attend such functions, but in an effort to find the right mate, he'd gone.

And if Ellen turned out to be someone he could seriously consider, the event would be well worth it.

Now Sunday was passing with agonizing slowness. He'd enjoyed last Saturday with Sunny. He wondered if she'd be interested in wandering around the wharf again, or maybe taking a hike in Golden Gate Park.

Dialing her number, the anticipation that built surprised him. He'd seen her last night and their parting had been less than satisfactory. Her attitude at the end of the evening should have put him off. Contrary creatures.

Instead, he wanted to talk to her, hear her prattle on about the party or a dress she was designing or the newest wedding she had promised to choreograph.

He could ask her more questions about Ellen, find out more about the woman who might one day be his wife.

Her phone rang endlessly.

Reluctantly Tanner hung up.

Was she out with Joe? The thought burned. He had no right to be jealous of her time when not with him. She was merely helping him out in exchange for relief on the loan from his company.

If he didn't have that hold over her, would she spend any time with him? Would she willingly help him find the kind of wife he wanted?

He sheered away from guessing the answer, knowing he probably wouldn't like it.

Tanner wandered around his living room, crossing to the window to stare out at the clear blue sky.

There were things he could do. Accounts at the office that he could study.

His mind went blank.

There was nothing else.

For the first time in years he had nothing he wanted to do, except talk to Sunny. The attraction of work paled. He had few outside interests, few friends. Goal-oriented since his childhood, he'd set a target and pushed forward until he achieved it.

But leisure time hadn't been important. He had no hobbies, no burning interests aside from work. And now his goal of marriage and a son. Or daughter, as Sunny had suggested.

For a moment a smile touched his lips. He could envision a bundle of energy with blond hair and bright blue eyes running up to him to share something, a new dolly, or a picture she'd drawn. He'd study it gravely and announce that it was perfect. As that precious little girl would be.

Turning away in disgust, he frowned. He wasn't planning to make a baby with Sunny. She didn't fit his vision of the perfect wife.

Yet the image of Sunny as she'd been last night rose. Sleek, sophisticated, polished. She held her own with every other woman there. Even her normal exuberance had been dampened, until she personified his ideal woman, his image for a wife.

But it was false.

That wasn't the real Sunny. The woman he was coming to know was casual and spontaneous, embracing everything life had to offer with wild abandon. Kicking off her shoes whenever possible, she didn't pretend to be sophisticated and blasé about life. Instead, she sallied forth with enthusiasm and childlike delight.

And for a few hours, whenever in her company, she opened the world to him in a way he'd never seen before.

She was different, that was it. A novelty.

He'd grow tired of it after a while.

She expected more from him than he wanted to give. His world was ordered, just the way he wanted it. He'd worked hard to achieve all he had, now it was time to move to the next stage, a marriage alliance that would cement his achievements and assure his acceptance in the society of the city.

But he wasn't married yet, and if he wanted to spend more time with Sunny Pritchard, he'd darn well do so.

He pulled his phone from his pocket and punched in her number. He hadn't achieved all he had by giving up easily. And he didn't plan to give up on reaching Sunny today, either.

By nine that night, Tanner finally admitted defeat. He'd tried calling her every fifteen minutes throughout the afternoon and evening. Obviously she wasn't answering her phone. Did she know he was trying to call and ignoring him?

Or had she left her phone at home when she went out?

If she'd gone out when would she be home? For all he knew she planned to spend the night away from home. And if so, who with?

Jealousy simmered just below the surface.

And anger.

And a bit of frustration that she didn't care to spend her afternoon with him.

He knew she'd enjoyed last weekend, that was one thing he liked about her, she didn't dissemble. She let people know instantly if she liked or disliked something.

Monday morning Tanner called the boutique. Eve answered the phone.

"Sunny, please," Tanner said, settling back, anticipating her voice.

"Sorry, she's busy right now. May I take a message?"

"This is Tanner Wright."

"Can I help you? Or take a message for Sunny?"

Did her voice sound cautious?

Used to reading people when making deals involving vast amounts of money, he paid strict attention.

"When she's free, have her call me."

"Um, that might be quite a while. Is there anything I can do?"

"I'll wait for her call."

Tanner wasn't going to be fobbed off with Sunny's assistant. He wanted Sunny. He hung up. What was up with the woman?

Ten minutes later Rachel put through a call from Eve.

"Mr. Wright, Sunny asked me to let you know she's going to be tied up most of the day and asked if I'd call you. If there is anything urgent, maybe I could help?"

"Doing what?"

"I beg your pardon?"

"What is Sunny doing all day that she can't take five minutes to return a call?"

"Um, we have a full schedule today. If there is anything I can do, please let me know. Sunny said to tell you good luck with Ellen."

Eve said a polite goodbye.

Tanner swore softly. Staring at the phone he wondered if he even wanted to call Ellen. She'd seemed a perfect candidate on Saturday night, but he was more interested in Sunny at the moment. From her odd attitude Saturday, to being away from home all day yesterday, to this latest development something was going on, but what?

He hit redial and waited. Eve answered again.

"Tell Sunny I want to speak to her this morning. If I don't hear from her, the deal changes. All bets off. Tell her that."

He hung up before Eve could say a word. It took longer than he had expected to get the call. Rachel buzzed him just prior to lunch.

"Sunny Pritchard on line two," she said efficiently.

Glancing at his watch, he saw it was almost noon.

"Cutting it a bit close, aren't you?" he said when he made the connection.

"I'm busy. What do you want?" Anger shimmered across the lines.

"I wanted to talk to you."

"So just because you want to talk, my life has to go on hold? I'm supposed to drop everything? Who do you think you are?"

"The man who holds the note on your business," Tanner replied coolly.

The silence fairly seethed.

"Are you free for lunch?" he asked.

"No."

Tanner waited, surprised that a torrent of words that wasn't forthcoming. Sunny usually talked forever.

"Sunny—"

"Look, Tanner. I am really busy. I don't have time to stop and pander to your whim for lunch. Call Ellen. You have her number. I have to go. Do what you want about the note."

The phone disconnected.

It would serve her right if he called the note today.

But he wouldn't. He preferred to have Sunny owe him. That way he'd have a reason to see her again.

He flicked the paper with Ellen's phone number on it. He'd hold off another day before calling her.

Tanner rang the doorbell. Dressed in jeans and a pullover shirt, he hoped he was casual enough to suit his snippy friend. He glanced at the leather running shoes. Probably too formal. Maybe he should try the bare-footed look.

Sunny opened the door, surprise clearly evident on her face. Was there also a trace of joy? He couldn't be sure. Instantly she masked her expression, blanking all emotion from her face.

"I wasn't expecting you," she said.

He smiled. Always catch the opposition off guard had been a maxim of his for years.

"May I come in?"

He raised the flowers and handed them to her. The smile that lit her eyes couldn't be blanked out, he thought gratefully.

"They're lovely," she murmured as she slowly reached for the bouquet.

Relief was almost tangible. He'd taken a risk buying daisies and carnations rather than roses.

But he wasn't here for hearts and flowers, he'd come to visit a friend. Every woman loved flowers, and when he'd passed the vendor on the corner, he couldn't resist. Sunny's smile was worth the unusual impulse.

"I guess you're staying?" she asked, looking over the colorful display.

He nodded.

"Have a seat, I'll put them in water."

If he didn't know better, he'd think she was flustered. Ignoring her invitation, he followed her into the kitchen. He leaned against the doorjamb, watching her hunt for a large vase.

"Why are you here?" she asked when she found one in the far back corner of a cupboard. Running water in it, she kept her eyes carefully averted from Tanner.

"I wanted to see you," he said easily.

"Why?"

"Beats me. You've been in a bad mood for days."

She shrugged, arranging the flowers in the vase to suit her, a slow smile tugging at her lips.

Tanner wanted to feel that smile against his own mouth, wanted to gather her up and kiss her until they both had trouble breathing. He wanted to feel her feminine body pressed tightly against his, taste her sweetness, savor the fragrance that surrounded her. Capture some of the heat and excitement and very essence of Sunny Pritchard.

He folded his arms across his chest and took a breath. Not yet. Maybe later, but first he was going to get to the bottom of her weird behavior.

"Business is brisk apparently," he murmured.

"Yes."

She fussed with the flowers until he wanted to take the bunch and toss them in the sink. Maybe they hadn't been such a good idea after all. He wanted her to look at him, not the stupid blossoms.

"Did you get your accounts in order?"

Sunny looked over the flowers as she turned, holding the vase as if a shield.

"Is that why you came tonight? To check up on my books?"

"No."

She walked toward him, her expression wary.

Tanner debated remaining exactly as he stood. He wondered if she'd push against him to move him or stop and keep her distance. Curious, he nevertheless moved aside and let her pass.

Her distinctive fragrance filled the air. His fingers clenched into a tight fist to keep from reaching out to thread through her soft hair, to touch that velvet skin.

"So why did you come tonight?" she asked as she settled the vase on the table in the living room.

Soft music played in her stereo, a book had been laid face down on the floor beside her chair.

"To see you."

"Did you call Ellen?" she asked, standing in front of the window.

There was little that welcomed him. She was rigid and wary.

"Not yet."

He sat on her sofa and stared at her.

"Are you going to stand there all night?"

Shaking her head, she moved to sit on the chair, tucking her feet beneath her. Tonight they were covered in bright yellow socks. There were no shoes in evidence.

"Why haven't you called Ellen?"

"No rush, is there?"

"I thought you were in a rush. I thought you wanted to get settled before your next birthday or something."

Did he imagine an almost imperceptible thawing?

"It'd be nice, but not earth-shattering if I don't make it. Some things take time."

"Ellen's nice."

"So you say. Tell me about how busy you've been this week."

She fidgeted with the edge of her shirt.

"Lots of people are planning weddings in the next few months. I've been recommended by several former clients who had very successful ones. Things are picking up."

She glanced up suddenly.

"If you don't foreclose soon, I think I'll be able to make a big payment on the loan. If you are worried about losing money on the deal, you can rest assured that you won't."

He nodded gravely.

"Thank you, I'll sleep better knowing that."

She frowned, then laughed softly.

"As if the few thousand lousy bucks your company lent me are more than a drop in your bucket. I can't imagine you losing sleep over something like that. In fact, I bet you sleep fine every night."

"Mostly."

He settled back, stretching his legs out, tucking his hands behind the waistband of his jeans. Resting his head on the back of her sofa, he half closed his eyes and watched her. A deep feeling of contentment slowly permeated.

"Made up any new expensive dresses that people aren't buying?" he asked lazily.

She shook her head.

"That dress is gorgeous. It'll sell someday. And I've taken your wise words to heart—now I ask for a hefty deposit and will have the complete dress paid for by the final fitting. See what a good student I've proved to be?"

"Until someone comes along who can't afford something, and your soft heart gives away the store."

"You're so cynical. A wedding's a special time for a woman. Romantic and precious. I hate to intrude with the crassness of money."

"Yet if you don't, you won't be able to make their wedding dreams come true because you'll be out of business."

"Logical as well as cynical. Do you practice that or did it come naturally? Joe is the same way, about some things."

"I don't want to talk about Joe," Tanner said firmly.

She smiled, amusement dancing in her eyes.

"Jealous?"

"Do you want me to be?"

Laughing gently, Sunny shook her head.

"I guess not And there's no reason to be, even if you were interested in me, which of course you're not. You want someone like Ellen. Right? Or Carmella if she didn't brag about money. Or maybe Julie if she could be coerced into a bit more modesty about her volunteer work."

"Or maybe I haven't met the right woman yet."

She blinked.

"Really? What other requirements do you want? I thought we went through everything."

"Do you think Ellen would be most suitable?"

Sunny hesitated a moment, her gaze dropping to her hand where she fiddled with the shirt hem again.

"I suppose. "

"But she wasn't one of the ones you invited to lunch."

"She's a bit quiet. I thought you needed someone a bit more lively. Carmella loves to entertain and Julie is quite polished that way. Ellen is more of a homebody. Which would be fine for you, I guess. Didn't you say you wanted your wife to stay home with your children?"

"Yes."

"That would be nice. I mean a lot of women would love to do that. Of course, you have to realize some of that comes from your own mother being gone when you were a child. If a woman isn't happy staying at home, doing so won't make it a good experience for the children. Lots of women work now, you know, and still raise healthy well-adjusted children. And you'll have a very strong, positive influence in your kids' lives."

"I plan to spend a lot of time with them."

"Don't push them to do everything you wished you could have done as a child. I see that a lot, especially in wedding planning. The mother of the bride always wished for more than what she had as a bride and tries to get it through her daughter. A wedding should be so very personal between the bride and groom, not a manifestation of her mother's dreams."

"I don't plan to try to relive my childhood through my children."

"Good."

He watched her, knowing she couldn't keep still, or silent, for long.

"You look awfully relaxed," she said a moment later.

"I feel relaxed. You're easy to be with."

"Maybe you should practice being relaxed with Ellen."

"Maybe Ellen isn't the right one."

Sunny sighed.

"Honestly, Tanner, you have to make some sort of effort with this project. I can't do everything."

"Some projects take time."

"Why did you come here tonight?"

"I wanted to see you."

"Oh."

She shifted in the chair, glanced at him, glanced away.

Tanner's amusement grew as her uncertainty and squirming increased.

"Did you want to talk about anything in particular?" she asked.

"No. Do you?"

"I could tell you about work. Or you could tell me about your work. Or we could talk about other women who might be suitable candidates for your wife."

"Or we could talk about something else. Is my finding a wife all that is between us?"

"What else could there be?"

"Friendship?" he suggested.

"For how long?"

"How long do you keep friends? Sean and I have been friends for seventeen years. I expect we'll stay friends for life."

"You want us to be friends for life?"

"Would that be a problem?"

Suddenly he wanted her to commit to being his friend for life. He wanted to know he could count on her throughout the years, no matter who he married, no matter what happened with her shop. He wanted some certainty for the future. Would she give it?

"I don't know," she hedged.

"Come and sit beside me, Sunny."

Tanner patted the cushion beside him. Every part of her appeared to go on alert. She became still, her eyes widened.

"Why?"

Smiling slowly, he patted the sofa. His immediate urge was to yank her from that chair and into his arms, but he'd pursue her slowly, cautiously. He wanted her tonight and he always got what he wanted. Sunny was a babe in arms when compared to him.

She studied him and Tanner wished he had access to her thoughts. He could almost see the vacillation, the arguments for and against moving. Finally, she huffed a short sigh and rose, crossing the room to sit beside him, watching him as warily as a rabbit would watch a wolf.

He reached his hand out and caught her, entwining their fingers. Leaning back again, he closed his eyes. Better to lure her into a feeling of safety before he moved to the next step.

"Tell me about the weddings you planned this week."

When given a topic near and dear to her heart, Sunny could go on forever. Slowly, at first, she offered tidbits of her workday, growing in enthusiasm and excitement as he nodded in understanding as she explained the various aspects of complex wedding plans, from scheduling sought-after churches and dealing with fussy caterers, to the intricacies of accessories for the bride and her attendants.

Tanner listened to her voice, enjoying the rich melodious tones as she expounded on her work. A man could do a lot worse than come home to someone like Sunny each day.

Startled at the trend of his thoughts, he opened his eyes and looked at her. Silky blond curls swirled around her face, a hint of pink tinged her cheeks, her blue eyes sparkled and shone.

He tugged and she leaned closer, her sentence trailing off as her gaze locked with his, as she read the intent and desire he knew must be blazing in his eyes.

9

She stopped talking.

He could see her swallow hard, her eyes questioning. Slowly he pulled her even closer, releasing her hand to encircle her. He wanted her in his embrace. He wanted to touch her, had shown outstanding restraint to wait this long.

One hand cupped her chin. He traced his thumb along her jaw, brushing across her pink lips. They opened slightly and his heart kicked into high gear. Lowering his face, he kissed her. There was no response. Pulling back a fraction, he gazed down into her confused eyes.

"Sunny?"

Smoothing the soft skin over her cheek, he watched the expressions chase around her face.

"I don't think this is such a good idea," she said softly.

"Why not?"

"I thought you were interested in Ellen."

"I enjoyed meeting her. Maybe I'll call her and see if she'd like to go out. But tonight I came to see you."

"Why?"

"Why not, aren't we friends?"

He brushed his lips across hers once. Twice. She was so soft, so delightfully feminine. He wanted—

"I don't think we're friends."

She leaned against his hands, but he didn't release her.

"I thought we were more like business associates."

"And friends."

He threaded his fingers in the silkiness of her hair and tilted her head slightly for better access. When he covered her mouth with his this time, she gave a soft sigh and responded. Her lips met his with a will all their own.

When he moved to deepen the kiss, she opened her mouth and he tasted the honey sweetness. He slipped his arm around her, drawing her up against his chest, reveling in the differences between their bodies, reveling in the feelings that surged through him when she pressed against him.

He kissed her until they both longed for breath. Breaking apart, he smoothed her hair, brushed the fire in her cheeks. Her lips were rosy and slightly swollen.

"That's nice."

She shoved against his chest and pushed herself to her feet.

"Maybe too nice. You need to leave, Tanner. This roller-coaster ride is too much for me. I fulfilled my part of the bargain. You need to remember your goal. It isn't to kiss up some *friend*, it's to get yourself your perfect wife, remember?"

"And does one preclude the other?" he asked lazily.

His manner was deceptive. Every cell in his body raged to hold her again, to kiss her, make her his.

But he had not succeeded in the cutthroat business of investing by showing the opposition his every thought.

What was Sunny's problem?

"What about me?" she asked.

"What about you?"

He stood and crossed the room to stand beside her. He fisted his hands, resisting the strong urge to gather her up again and resume their kiss.

"Maybe I don't want to be a substitute."

"A substitute? What are you talking about? I don't see you as some sort of substitute—for what?"

"You should be out romancing the woman you plan to marry, not kissing me."

She turned away, dragging her fingers through her hair.

"I'm busy, Tanner, and not up to games right now. Take your killer kisses and give them to your trophy bride."

"Killer kisses, huh?"

He reached for her shoulders, planning to turn her back to face him, but the tension that hummed through her body startled him. Slowly he massaged the tight muscles, lowering his head to rest beside hers.

Softly he spoke.

"I like the sound of killer kisses, want to share some more?"

"No. I want you to leave."

He spun her around at the note in her voice, shocked to see tears shimmering in her eyes.

"Sunny, what's wrong?"

"This is all wrong, that's what. I shouldn't be trying to find you a wife, you should find your own. And you shouldn't settle for less than what everyone deserves, love and caring. Buying yourself some sophisticated woman to complement your lifestyle is plain dumb. And I'm not going to be a part of it. I can't. I wish this had never started. I was much happier before."

She sniffed, and brushed her eyes with her fingertips, but the tears spilled over and ran down her cheeks.

Tanner felt a touch of panic. He hadn't a clue how to handle a crying woman. He remembered his mother crying once, and how helpless he felt as a child. The same feeling swamped him.

"Don't cry, Sunny."

He hugged her, holding her as she struggled for control.

"I'll be fine. I'm tired, that's all. Just leave, please."

She wiped her cheeks again and tried a smile. It didn't make it, but he gave her credit for the effort. But the entreaty in her eyes reached him.

"I'll call you."

"Don't. Take Ellen out and give her a real chance. She's a person who wants to be loved as much as anyone. Don't shortchange her or yourself by denying the possibility. And if she's not the one you want, wait until you find the right one."

"Love's fine for some romantic woman like you, wrapping yourself up in weddings and brides and lace and satin. But it's been in short supply in my life, and I'm not waiting the rest of my days for it to magically appear. I make my own way in this world, and I'll form my own family."

"And love them?"

"Any children, certainly."

"And your wife?"

"After time I'm sure I'll grow fond of her."

"That is the coldest thing I've ever heard. Goodbye, Tanner. Good luck with your business marriage."

She stormed to the door and flung it wide, standing beside it, refusing to look at him. When he reached the opening, he tilted her face again, to meet his eyes.

"I'll send Stuart over tomorrow to check out the books and help you set up your accounts. Did you call your suppliers about a quantity discount?"

"I said I would, didn't I?"

"Just checking. I don't leave much to chance, too many screw ups happen if I don't follow up."

"I'm not your responsibility," she said, her teeth clamped tightly together.

"Just protecting my investment," he said smoothly.

Dropping a light kiss against her mouth, he walked down the hallway, wincing when he heard her door slam shut behind him. He wondered idly if the neighbors were used to it or was this a first.

He bet she never slammed the door behind Joseph Thurmond Sanger the Fourth.

At least he knew tonight she hadn't been with her friend Joe. It eased the burning in his chest a little.

"Got a minute?" Stuart stood in the door to Tanner's office the next afternoon.

"Sure, come in. What's up?" Tanner leaned back in his chair and motioned his chief accountant to a chair.

"About Sunny Pritchard's business. You asked me to send someone over there to set her up with proper accounts. I sent Nancy Brewer. She got back a little while ago. Apparently your friend Ms. Pritchard has decided she doesn't need our help."

"What?"

"She politely but very firmly told Nancy to take a hike. Nancy did as she was told and left."

"Any reasons given?" Tanner asked.

"Just that she had been managing her business since she started and she didn't need any help now, thank you very much."

"She's going to run it into the ground the way she's going. And she most definitely needs some help to get the mess straightened out. It's my investment I'm protecting," Tanner said.

"Let me know if you want me to send Nancy out again."

"Right."

Tanner waited until Stuart left before reaching for the phone. Sunny's attitude was beginning to annoy him.

Eve answered. Déjà vu, Tanner thought.

"I want to speak to Sunny."

"She's not here."

Gone was the helpful attitude that had marked her earlier reception.

"When do you expect her?"

"Not until tomorrow. I'll tell her you called, if you like," Eve said.

"Is she home?"

"Not that I know of. She had business to take care of. That's all she said, so you can ask a dozen questions, but I truly don't know."

"Tell her to call me when you hear from her, would you?"

Tanner hung up after obtaining Eve's assurance she'd let Sunny know he'd called.

He dialed her home, got an answering machine. Was that new? He called her cell, it rang and rang.

And what game was she playing now? He'd told her he

planned to send an accountant. She didn't argue with him about it. Why the refusal to allow Nancy to set up her books?

Glancing at his calendar, he noted there was nothing after his two o'clock appointment.

Afterward, he'd take a quick drive to Union Street to see if Sunny had returned. If she hadn't, maybe he could get some information from Eve.

When he walked into the boutique, Tanner felt the same as he'd experienced once before—like a stranger in an alien place. The ruffles and lace setting remained foreign to him, made to suit the fancy of women at their most romantic.

He studied the lovely dress on the mannequin while he waited for someone to realize he was there. Even a man could realize how fancy it was and how it could represent the fantasy every woman wanted for a wedding day.

For a moment he wondered about his own parents' wedding. Had his mother worn such a dress? Had she and his father been full of dreams and plans for a wonderful future? Or had it been a hurried-up affair, hastily planned and hastily executed?

He'd never know. There was no one left to tell him. He never saw a wedding picture, nor signs of a fancy dress like this. And he'd been so young when she left. His father had never spoken kindly about his wife once she was gone.

The dress looked small. He bet it would fit Sunny like a glove. Had she tried it on when it first arrived? Or maybe after the client had canceled the order?

He could envision her wearing it. The lace would be

beautiful against her skin, the soft white tone virginal and ethereal. Would she wear her hair in the froth of curls or slick it back into some elaborate style to suit a special occasion? He knew she'd be barefoot beneath the long skirt. Even on her wedding day.

He'd be willing to make a large bet on that.

"Hello, Mr. Wright. Sunny still hasn't returned. I really don't expect her today."

Eve came from the back, stood behind the counter as if putting a barrier between them. For a moment Tanner wondered if she felt safer or more in control with the solid wood and glass to hide behind.

"I sent an accountant over this morning to see about setting up the business's accounts," he said.

"Sunny doesn't need help there, she said," Eve replied. "And I do believe it is still her business. She gets to make the decisions."

"It won't be her business for long if she runs it into the ground because of sloppy accounting practices."

Frustrated, Tanner glared at the woman.

"I wouldn't know about that. Sunny handles her own business affairs. Was there something else?"

A hint of antagonism colored her voice.

"I tried her home and her cell, she's not answering anywhere."

Eve remained silent, her eyes gravely studying him.

"Do you know where she is?"

She shook her head. "No."

"Why did she take off after sending Nancy away?"

"She only said she had to see a man about a loan. I thought she was going to see you until you called."

See a man about a loan? Had she come to the office after he left? Was she looking for him even as he stood here searching for her?

Tanner stepped back near the door and punched in his office number.

"Rachel, did Sunny Pritchard stop by this afternoon?"

"No, boss. Was she expected? I don't have her noted on the calendar."

"I wasn't expecting her, just thought she might have stopped by. Or called?"

"No."

"I'll be back within the hour if she does call."

Tanner saw the special delivery envelope as soon as he entered his office.

"I put that on your desk. The messenger said it was urgent," Rachel said, following him to the door of his office. "It was marked personal, so I didn't open it."

"Thanks, Rachel."

She smiled and nodded, pulling the door closed to give him privacy.

Shrugging out of his suit jacket, Tanner tossed it across a chair. He picked up the envelope, mentally reviewing all the deals that were cooking. Nothing of such immediacy came to mind. He slit the envelope and drew out a letter, and a check.

Dear Tanner:

Enclosed is a check in the full amount that Brides and Bows owes your firm. I consider our business association ended. Best of luck in finding your perfect wife. Sincerely,

Sunny Pritchard

He glanced at the cashier's check. He'd have to get Stuart to run a balance, but it looked as if it was made out for the full amount.

"Hell's bells, Sunny, what do you think you're doing?" he murmured as he stared at the letter again.

Where had she gotten the money? It was a hefty sum, not easily raised. Certainly no bank would have advanced her the money—not based on her track record and the deplorable state of her books.

And why?

He walked to the window and gazed out over the office buildings of San Francisco.

Why had she so abruptly severed their relationship? Had he come on too strongly last night?

She'd kissed him back.

Then cried.

He thought they were developing a friendship. He'd never had one with a woman before and it proved to be a novel experience.

Had he misread the signs? He didn't think so.

Sending a letter and a check wasn't the way to end a friendship. She should have at least had the decency to confront him in person.

He'd fix that. He spun around and crossed to his desk, reaching for the phone.

By nine-thirty that night, Tanner was about to give up. He'd called Sunny's numbers all afternoon and evening. Voice mail responded each time. He'd tried to tone down his anger. At least after the first five or six messages. Where was she?

Reaching the end of his patience, he searched his contacts to look up Sean's number. In seconds he had his friend on the phone.

Hi, what's up?"

"Do you know where Sunny is?"

"Was it my turn to watch her?" Sean asked jovially.

"This is serious. Do you know where she is?"

Tanner was in no mood for jokes He wanted to find Sunny.

"No. What's wrong? I guess she's home."

"She's not answering her phone. And she's not at Brides and Bows. I need to find her."

"What's going on with the two of you? I thought Sunny was helping you filter out your perfect wife," Sean said. "Yet at Toddy's party, you showed up as Sunny's date. That's after coming together to Mom's house that Sunday for the barbecue. And after I heard about you and Sunny having lunch at the London Pub."

"She's doing just what you said, introducing me to prospective candidates. But we've run into a snag and I need to get in touch with her."

"If she isn't home, she's probably out on a date. Catch her tomorrow."

"Tonight," Tanner insisted.

Sean didn't speak for a long moment.

"If you are pulling one of your business deals where my cousin gets the short end—"

"I'm not pulling anything. We had an agreement—never mind. I just want to talk to Sunny, as soon as possible."

"She could be on a date."

"I don't think so. She left work early and hasn't been home, as far as I can tell."

"You've been trying to reach her?"

"All afternoon. She's not answering her cell or the land line at her apartment. Eve said she left the shop and didn't tell her where she was going."

"She must be busy, then. She likes to talk to people on the phone You know she can run on a bit."

"I wouldn't have guessed," Tanner said dryly.

Sean chuckled.

"She's a wonderful person."

"I agree. See if you can find out where she is, will you, Sean?"

"Right. I'll call you back when I find out something."

"I'm at the office. I'm leaving in a few minutes."

"Sounds like Sunny had the right of it, lecturing you on your workaholic tendencies."

"Yeah, maybe so. Call me if you find out where she is."

Tanner drove from the office to Sunny's apartment. The windows were dark. He didn't bother to go up.

While he could see her refusing to answer the phone, letting the answering machine respond to make sure she didn't answer his call, he couldn't picture her sitting alone in the dark all night.

She wasn't home.

Giving up temporarily, he headed home. Sean hadn't called yet. He tossed his suit coat on the back of the sofa and headed for the kitchen. A sandwich would tide him over. How long before Sean called?

At midnight Tanner called Sean.

"What did you find out?"

"Nothing, I said I'd call you when I had something. I checked with a few friends, no one's seen her. It was already late when you called. It wouldn't be worth my life to call Aunt Susan or my mom so late unless it was an emergency. I'll check with them in the morning. I said I'd call you when I heard something. Hey, man, what's up? I've never seen you push so hard for something like this."

"Just tying up some loose ends," Tanner hedged.

No sense telling Sean the entire story, at least until he himself figured out what it was. He hung up the phone.

On the table was the paper on which he'd scribbled Ellen's phone number. He picked it up and crushed it into a ball.

Why would he want to date Ellen Naylor when he could spend time with Sunny?

In fact, who was he kidding that he wanted some sleek sophisticated woman to be his wife?

He wanted Sunny.

It was time to forget his elaborate, sterile plan to find a paragon of a wife like some men bought racehorses. Before Sunny, he thought the plan a sound one. Now he wanted more.

He wanted a warm, loving woman to come home to. Wanted to finish work early so he could share dinner and the tasks leading up to the meal. Wanted to spend evenings together, talking about their days, planning for a long future.

He wanted Sunny in that future, to fascinate him with her chatter, to bring a balance to his own narrow focus on life. Her rosy view of life differed drastically, maybe he could counter balance her views. Together they could be stronger than each was alone.

He loved Sunny Pritchard!

Tanner pitched the balled paper into a trash can and headed for the kitchen. He needed a drink, a strong one. And then he'd look at the obvious. How long had he been in love with her?

After a lifetime of denying there was such an emotion as love, of being convinced that it didn't exist, he'd fallen under its spell almost without being aware of it. He couldn't imagine a future with another woman. He wanted Sunny.

One thing he prided himself on was the ability to move with the flow, when deals turned, he was quick to react, quick to formulate new strategy and move in a new direction. He could do the same with his life.

First he'd find Sunny. Then tell her he loved her. Surely she loved him in return.

He reached for a glass and the whiskey bottle. Taking a sip of the amber liquid, he contemplated the possibility that she did not.

She hadn't been anxious to help him find a possible life mate, yet that had not been from any selfish self-interest, but merely her belief that his stated goal was a poor reason to marry.

Turns out she was right.

She'd spent time with him, but always with the end goal of finding him a bride, another woman for his bride. She didn't approve of many facets of his life, from his long working hours to his cold way of analyzing a relationship and moving toward his goal.

He wasn't perfect. The more he thought about it, the less he found to make him suspect she loved him. She'd certainly pointed out how crazy she thought his goal of finding the perfect wife was.

Sunny wouldn't be perfect, either. She'd probably drive him crazy a dozen times a year.

But she'd also perfect his world, bringing sunshine and laughter where there had only been work and more work and long dreary nights.

They'd started building a friendship, spent many hours together companionably. He could be patient, wait for her to fall in love with him. Do things she liked. He was good at strategic planning. He could figure out what she wanted and make sure she got it.

Somehow along the way he had to make sure she knew he no longer wanted another woman. That she'd been right, his way of acquiring a wife was wrong.

But would she fall in love with him?

He wasn't Joseph Thurmond Sanger the Fourth. He didn't have a family name worth a hill of beans.

He had some money, but she seemed singularly unimpressed with wealth.

That led to his wondering for the one hundredth time where she'd gotten the money today to pay off the loan from Wright Associates.

Pacing a path in the living room carpet, he sipped the drink, remembering all the hours he'd spent with Sunny. How could he not have suspected where they were heading? He'd dated plenty of women casually, with no ties, no expectations.

But he never dressed casually and went to their apartments merely to listen to them talk about their job.

Never went to family parties.

Never spent a day wandering around San Francisco, eating at the tourist traps and riding the cable cars.

And never before felt so lost and found in the blue of a woman's eyes.

"Where the hell are you, Sunny?" he asked aloud.

Tanner was still home the next morning when his phone rang. He'd dressed in jeans and a casual shirt. He didn't plan to go into the office—not until he found Sunny and talked with her.

"You sorry bastard, what did you do to her?"

Sean's accusing voice sounded in Tanner's ear when he picked up the phone.

"I didn't do anything. What did she say I did?"

"Nothing to me, I told you I didn't know where she was. But I've found out quite a bit and want to know what you did to chase her away."

Tanner gripped the receiver tightly, but kept his voice cool.

"I am rather curious about that myself. I saw her night before last, the next thing I knew, she sends me a check for the full amount of the investment Wright's made and told me she could no longer help find me a wife."

"What else?"

Tanner could almost feel the heat of Sean's anger.

"Nothing else."

"I'm not buying it. Sunny's never before felt she had to leave town over something."

"Leave town?"

"And she borrowed some money from Theo. I can't imagine what she went through to do that. She always swore she wouldn't take his money, even though he offered to help her out many times. He's crazy about her and wants to do things for her like he does her mother."

"Theo, of course. I wondered where she got the money."

"Have you heard anything I've said? I want some answers and I want them now."

"Hold on, Sean. I told you, I don't know what is going on, that's why I want to talk with Sunny. Where is she?"

Sean hesitated.

"Come on, Sean. I'm not going to hurt her. I just want to talk to her."

"Why should I trust anything you say? You are apparently the reason she left. Why tell you where she's gone? Leave her alone, Tanner."

Tanner closed his eyes.

"Sean, I can't."

"Sure you can. Leave my cousin alone. Find your own trophy wife. You have enough background about the eligible women you've met. It was a dumb idea, I can't believe I even suggested it."

"I thought at first you were setting me up with your cousin," Tanner said slowly, opening his eyes.

He remembered seeing Sunny for the first time. Involuntarily he smiled.

"That would be like oil and water."

"Opposites attract."

"Right, you're saying you're attracted to Sunny?" Sean scoffed.

Tanner didn't respond.

"Tanner? You aren't saying you are attracted to Sunny?" Incredulity replaced the sarcasm.

"Yes, I am saying it. In fact I'll go one step farther than that, but only to Sunny."

"I don't believe this. You and Sunny? No wonder she ran."

"Where is she, Sean?"

If he didn't tell him, Tanner had no qualms about driving over to his place and finding a way to make him tell.

"Lake Tahoe. Theo's family has a huge home in Stateline. She went there to think things through. That's what she told her mother. I can't believe you fell for Sunny. She's not anything like Marie DuPont."

"I know. Except for the party last Saturday when she dressed to the nines, she's never fit my image of what I wanted. But it was just an image. She's real. And I want her."

Sean laughed.

"Good luck, pal. You're going to need it. I can't see Sunny giving in easily. Especially after whatever happened to drive her away."

"I don't know what drove her away. That's why I'm trying to find her, to discover what went wrong."

What went wrong beyond the obvious, having the woman he wanted assigned the task of locating a wife for him. He'd been a fool.

Sean gave him directions to the house at Lake Tahoe and told Tanner to call him when he returned to the city. He wanted to know the outcome.

Taking time to pack a small bag, and make two quick stops, Tanner headed for Lake Tahoe. He'd find Sunny and get her to explain why she'd paid off the debt and why she'd left the city so precipitously.

And then maybe he'd figure out a way to introduce the idea of the two of them seeing each other. Dating. With the end view the possibility of marriage. He hoped she'd at least listen to him.

He wasn't sure what he'd do if she didn't.

It was late by the time he reached Stateline. The motels and chalets, the shops and businesses that lined the road on the California side were busy. The high-rise buildings that comprised the casinos and hotels on the Nevada side reflected the setting sun in the myriad windows. He drove through the busy street, wondering if it was ever quiet in this town. Two miles beyond the strip he found the road Sean had named.

Turning, he followed it down to the lake, then along the water's edge until he found the house. There was a small car parked in the driveway. He realized he didn't know what kind of car she drove. There were a million other facts about her he didn't know yet.

Discovering everything about her would prove fascinating, of that he was sure.

If she'd let him.

There was still that.

10

Sunny opened the door at his knock. Upon recognizing him, she tried to slam it shut. Tanner stuck his foot in the opening, insuring she couldn't lock him out.

"I want to talk to you," he said, his hand gripping the edge of the door, pushing against it until she gave up and stepped back.

"I'd think you would get a hint that I don't want to talk to you. Who told you I was here? Sean, I bet. How did he find out? I might have known my male cousin would bond with his male friend and throw his female relative to the wolves."

"Wolves?"

Tanner raised an eyebrow.

The relief at finding her dimmed a bit at the obvious lack of welcome in her eyes.

In fact, he looked closer, she looked as if she'd been crying again.

"So am I cast as the big bad wolf?"

She shrugged.

"If the shoe fits," she said, turning away, giving up on an attempt to shut him out.

Tanner took advantage and stepped inside, closing the door behind him. He followed her into the spacious living room. For a moment the breathtaking view from the huge picture window drew his attention.

The snow-covered mountains that rimmed Lake Tahoe were silhouetted in the dying rays of the sun, the lake dark and mysterious in the evening shadows. But the grandeur of the scene couldn't be hidden by the darkness. It was spectacular. He'd like to see the view in all seasons and all times of the day.

"Nice view," he commented, shifting his gaze to Sunny.

Beautiful as it was, it didn't compare with the woman before him.

"Came with the house," she said flippantly. "What are you doing here?"

She glared at him.

"I came to talk to you."

"I don't have anything to say. I sent you a check for the full amount I owed your company. Our association is ended."

"Wasn't there more between us than business, Sunny?" he asked.

If she didn't feel anything for him, his task would be all the harder. But he was used to overcoming tremendous odds to succeed. He'd done it in business, he'd do it with his personal life.

He wanted her at his side the rest of his life. He'd do whatever it took to achieve that end.

She looked at him warily, suspicion forming in her face. "Like what?"

He wanted her to smile, to see the dancing light in her eyes, to have her exuberance back in full force.

What had gone wrong? And how could he get them back on track? Especially if she wasn't interested.

Now that the time was at hand, he became unsure. Unused to expressing his feelings, except anger, which he handled better each year, he was at a loss.

If she didn't care something for him, he'd look like a total idiot to hand her the weapon of his true feelings.

Yet someone had to make a move.

"How did you get the money to repay the loan?"

"That's not your affair," she said, watching him warily.

"Satisfy my curiosity."

"I asked Theo, he said yes."

He nodded and took a step closer.

"I thought you didn't want to take advantage of Theo's generosity and ask him for the start-up money."

"I didn't."

"But?"

"But he's always offered and I saw it as a way to end this farce between us."

She turned and gazed out the window. Tanner wondered if she saw the beauty of the scenery or was too caught up in the conversation to notice.

"I thought we had a good working relationship."

"Shows how much you know," she muttered.

He stepped closer. He could smell the fragrance of her hair, the sweet scent that was Sunny.

"I like you, Sunny. I like spending time with you."

"You spent time with me as a way to find your ideal wife," she said flatly.

"Not just for that. What about Saturday when we wandered around the city together?"

"I thought you were trying to one-up Joe."

He frowned. That had been part of the reason he'd asked her out.

Primarily he wanted to make sure she knew she could enjoy being with him more than being with Joe. He hated thinking about her with the doctor. The two of them had so much in common with mutual backgrounds and friends.

How could an outsider hope to compete?

But the day spent together had been fun. And the evenings. And the trip to her aunt's. Playing horseshoes. Everything he'd done with her had been fun. It was Sunny's special gift, making the most mundane task an exciting adventure.

"I wanted to spend the day with you. It had nothing to do with Joseph Thurmond Sanger," he lied.

"I can't imagine why."

"You can't be that dense. You're delightful to be around. Funny, witty. You fairly sparkle with an enthusiasm that's totally refreshing. And that emotion is missing from most of the people I know these days. Everyone else is deadly serious about things."

"Like you. Cutthroat business is the be all and end all, right?"

She moved nervously, flicking a quick glance his way, then looking back out the window.

"Not always."

Used to reading people, Tanner realized he didn't have that knack with Sunny. She threw him completely.

"Give me a break, Tanner. You employed those ends to finding a wife. You made a list of requirements, set a goal and then relentlessly pursued it."

"Not anymore."

"What does that mean? Did you call Ellen? Have you

already made plans for a wedding?"

She turned around, stark horror displayed on her face. She took a breath and looked at the ashes in the fireplace.

He laughed softly. Had that look meant something? He grabbed hold to the thought.

"Even the fastest worker in the world would find it a bit hard to meet a woman last Saturday night and arrange a marriage by now. I haven't called her. Probably won't ever have an occasion to call her."

"I thought she met your requirements."

"I've rethought those requirements, modified them a bit."

"Oh?"

She glanced at him in surprise. She motioned to the sofa.

"Do you want to sit down or something? Since you seem to be staying. I want to go on record I want you to leave, but I don't suppose my desires will be met. You're bigger than I am, I can't force you out, so the only choice left is to hear what you have to say and then maybe you'll leave."

"Desires are something else we can talk about. But maybe we should clear the air on the wife issue first."

"Definitely."

She sat primly on the edge of a chair near the massive stone fireplace. Tanner considered letting her remain there, but decided against it. He'd go for broke in this confrontation. He had his goal firmly in mind and he'd use all his negotiating skills to bring about the desired end.

But in the meantime, skills or not, he wanted her close. He wanted to hold her. Touch her. Connect with her.

Reaching for her hand, he pulled her up. Ignoring her exclamation, he stepped across to the sofa and sat down.

He sat her beside him, still holding his hand.

"So why are you here?" She asked.

Tanner smiled. Curiosity was better than rejection. Fire lit her eyes, her cheeks glowed with color.

"I'm not sure where to start," he said after a moment.

He wasn't sure he wanted to say anything.

What he wanted to do was pull her onto his lap and kiss her until dawn.

Share his hopes and dreams, learn more of hers. Bind her to him so completely she'd never wish to leave.

"Great, you track me down when I'm trying to avoid seeing you, insist you have to talk to me, then can't decide where to start. Just say what you think you have to say and leave."

"Your note and check surprised me," he began.

"I didn't want to be involved anymore," she said stiffly. "Find your own wife."

"It must have been hard to ask your stepfather for a loan when you had resisted so long."

She stared straight ahead, her profile all he could see. But he felt the stiffening in her body.

"You didn't have to do that."

"I wanted out of our deal. With no loan to Wright Associates, I'd be free."

"You could have said something. At least brought me the check, rather than send it by messenger."

She looked at him then, anger flashing in her blue eyes.

"In case it escaped your notice, I was trying to avoid you. Why do you think I came to Lake Tahoe? I knew you'd be on the phone or at my apartment. I was trying to avoid you. Wait until I get my hands on Sean. Family should count more than the old boy network. Get him to help you find a bride."

"I think he did. I know who I want to marry. And I know all about her background, not that it's important anymore. The question isn't who I want, but if she'll have me," he said slowly.

He looked at their linked hands, suddenly more nervous than he'd ever been, even when closing his first million-dollar deal.

Sunny tossed her head, turning away and pulled her hand from his.

"I'm glad for you. If you have your wife lined up, why are you here?"

"I said I know who I want to marry, who I want to live the rest of my life with. But I'm not sure she feels the same."

"Offer her enough money, or jewelry, or unlimited entertaining. Isn't that what you want in a wife?" she said.

"I thought I did, but something changed along the way. And I didn't quite realize how much I've changed until yesterday."

"Yesterday?"

She looked at him.

The curiosity in her gaze was heartening. He had her attention now. If he could glean some of her feelings before exposing all of his, he'd feel better about the outcome.

"When I got your letter and then couldn't reach you."

"What does that have to do with anything?"

"I went by the shop, you know. Eve said you were gone, but I wasn't sure if she was telling the truth or not."

"She was, I left as soon as I sent the check. I knew you'd be upset."

"Upset?" he asked mildly.

She didn't have a clue to how he'd felt.

"So you went to the shop. I hope you didn't intimidate Eve."

"Like I do you?"

She shrugged.

"I don't intimidate very easily."

"I have never intimidated you a minute in your life," he commented. "A rather interesting turn of events, when I think about it. You're probably the only person I can say that about."

"Let's not analyze everything to death. That's the businessman in you, I suppose. Or is it just a male thing? Things are the way they are," she snapped.

"I know, let's look at it through rosy glasses, seeing only the wonderful aspects of everything and ignoring anything that doesn't fit our picture of how things should be."

The glimmer of a smile touched her.

"I don't ignore everything that doesn't fit my picture," she defended.

"While I waited for Eve to come out from the back room, I studied that pretty wedding dress on the mannequin. The one you got stuck with. You'd look lovely in it. Have you ever tried it on?"

"The wedding dress? Sure. When the client canceled her order, I was so mad. Then I looked at the dress and couldn't resist trying it on. It's in my size, you know."

"And I bet you looked like a dream. Would you wear your hair in some elaborate style or like you normally do?"

"Oh, right, I'm going to wear an elegant wedding gown

with this mop of curls? I'd have it styled, romantic and old-fashioned. If I ever had an occasion to wear it for real, I mean. Which I don't. I can't believe you even glanced at the dress, much less imagined me in it."

"I imagine you in a lot of things."

And out of them, too, but he thought it prudent to refrain from mentioning that at this juncture.

"Like what?"

She was intrigued, he could see it. Now if he just didn't come on too fast. He wanted her to relax, consider what he planned to propose.

"I see us taking walks around the city during the nice weather, maybe riding the cable cars again. I see you at Christmas delightfully choosing presents for family and friends, excited about decorating a tree and following all the traditions of the holiday. I see you cooking dinner, reading a book curled up in a chair, with your feet bare."

He glanced down. Socks covered her toes, but there were no shoes in evidence.

"From you that's almost poetic. What's the catch?" she asked warily.

"No catch. I like thinking about you."

"In between thinking of who you'd like to marry, which socialite would be best suited for the honor of Mrs. Tanner Wright?"

He sighed. He knew this wouldn't be easy.

"Sometimes when a goal is made, all the facts aren't known. Reassessing the situation leads to change."

"Meaning?"

"Meaning, could we forget about looking for a paragon for a wife?"

She looked at him, her eyes wide and questioning.

"I like spending time with you," he continued.

The emotions in his chest threatened to burst through. Why didn't she say something? Was he making a hash of this? He took a breath, it was do or die time.

"Sunny, I want you to marry me."

Her gaze never wavered.

She stared at him as if he'd lost his mind.

Slowly tears welled up in her eyes. Oh, God, she was going to cry.

He hadn't meant to make her cry.

"Sunny, don't cry. If you don't want to, that's okay. No, it's not okay, but I can live with it. Maybe the idea will grow on you. Don't cry."

She blinked and one tear spilled down her cheek.

"You want to marry me?" she asked.

"Yes."

His thumb brushed away the errant tear. Her skin was as silky as ever. He could hardly contain his urge to taste that soft skin, to kiss her and hold her and never let her go.

"Why?"

"Why? Why does a man normally want to marry a woman? So she'll be his wife."

"Oh, Tanner."

She raised her eyes to the ceiling as if seeking inspiration. Looking back at him, she slowly shook her head.

Panic swamped him. She was refusing? She couldn't. He wanted her like he'd never wanted anything else.

More than the money that enabled him to turn his back on the kind of life he'd known as a child.

More than some kind of entry into society.

He would choose a life with Sunny any day over all the rest.

What he wasn't sure of was if he'd be able to live with her rejection.

"Don't say no just yet, listen to what I have to offer."

"Tanner, I don't want to be a trophy bride. I told you my feelings in this matter at the very beginning. They haven't changed just because you think I might be suitable."

"But you haven't heard all I have to—"

"You have tons of material things and more money than should be legal. But that's not enough," she said gently, tears still shimmering in her eyes.

"You are right. It's not enough. I want you to share my life, Sunny, not my money. To be home when I get home and nag me if I work late. Share tasks around the house, plan vacations together. Did you know I haven't had a real vacation in over ten years? I expect living with you would change that."

"Tanner, I want more."

"You want commitment and loyalty and faithfulness and—"

His voice closed up.

Staring at her for some idea of how she felt, he could only feel a deepening sense of panic. She wasn't going to marry him. She'd be kind when she said no, but he had nothing she wanted.

He only had himself to offer.

And that was nothing to compare with Joseph Thurmond Sanger the Fourth.

"And love, Tanner. I want love."

He took a breath.

"I can offer that, as well."

"What?"

He cleared his throat.

"I love you, Sunny. I'm not quite sure how it happened, but it's true. I love you."

Tears flooded again, but her smile grew huge. Confused, he tried to figure out what was happening.

"Are you crying or smiling?"

"Both."

She flung herself into his arms, her own encircling his neck tightly. When she rested her face against his, he felt the dampness of her tears.

"Don't cry," he repeated.

"I'm so happy, I can't help it. I love you, Tanner Wright. I've had a crush on you for years, heard all about you from Sean. I was thrilled when I got to meet you. But you never even saw me. You wanted sleek and sophisticated and that I'll never be."

"I don't know, you looked pretty sophisticated at the party last Saturday night."

"Oh, sure, once in a while I can do it, but it's not the real me, the twenty-four-hours-a-day me."

"No, it's not, and I wouldn't change a single thing about you. Say yes, Sunny. Marry me."

She pulled back a bit to look deep into his eyes.

"I love you. Of course I'll marry you."

"Just needed to be sure. One of the first rules of business is never to assume."

She laughed and brushed the tears from her cheeks.

"Goodness, what an adventure. Me tied up with a died-in-the-wool businessman. Next thing I'll know Brides and Bows will be franchised and have boutiques across the country."

"If that is what you want—"

"No, silly, I'm just joking. I like my own little shop. It suits me. I'll want to keep working after we get married."

"Ultimatums already?" he asked lazily.

The relief flooded every inch of him.

She was going to marry him. She loved him. He almost couldn't believe it. But she'd said yes and he'd hold her to it, no matter what.

Heck, they were right in Nevada, they could be married tomorrow. That would link them forever.

"Not really. Do you mind that I work?"

"No."

Right now he'd grant her anything.

She'd said yes.

"And when the kids come, I'll be able to take them to work. Of course I can cut back by then. Hire another assistant. Eve could be the manager."

"Already thinking ahead. Maybe you're more of a businesswoman than you think," he said. "How many kids are we planning?"

"Lots, don't you think? We're both only children, I missed having brothers and sisters. Of course Sean and Gloria came close."

"Lots it is, then."

"I love you, Tanner. I hated thinking about you courting someone like Carmella when I wanted you to court me. But I sure don't fit all the criteria you listed. And I thought you didn't believe in love."

"I thought so, too. There hasn't been a lot of it in my life, Sunny. But when I got your letter and then couldn't reach you, it brought home exactly what my life would be like if I didn't see you again. I knew it was love when I hated the thought of your having to go to Theo when you had fought against it for so long. I could practically feel the blow to your pride. I wish you had talked to me instead of throwing that note in my face."

"I didn't think I could. I was really hurting that you seemed to be interested in Ellen and couldn't see me for the furniture. Somehow, after that first lunch, I thought you and I were a team. Then when you arranged to get Ellen's number without me, the reality of the situation hit me. You could ask her out and never see me again. I just couldn't stand it. I had to get away. And make sure there was nothing to keep us connected. I didn't want to have to pretend to be happy at your marriage to another woman."

"Ah, so that explains your attitude after the party. I couldn't figure that out."

"I tried to hide it."

"You succeeded. Maybe in fifty years or so, I'll be able to figure you out without your telling me."

"Maybe. But then, where's the excitement and mystery?"

"I expect I'll always find it with you."

When he kissed her, Tanner felt as if he'd come home. The flighty, tousled, casual woman he loved bore little resemblance to the ideal woman he thought he wanted.

Instead, Sunny brought sunshine and warmth into his life, and he wouldn't trade that for anything.

Epilogue

"It's time," Sean said.

Tanner looked at him and nodded. He checked the tux one more time in the mirror.

"I'm as ready as I'll ever be," he said grimly, wishing she had agreed to the quick wedding he'd wanted in Nevada.

Sean chuckled.

"I thought you wanted to marry her."

"I want her as my wife. It's this wedding I'm not so sure about."

"Hey, Brides and Bows planned it from beginning to end. It should go like clockwork."

"I don't know why she couldn't have settled for a quick visit to a judge," Tanner grumbled.

But he should have known from the first that his romantic bride would settle for nothing less than the fairy-tale wedding of her dreams.

At least the waiting was over. The months since he'd proposed had seemed endless.

Only this last week when they began moving Sunny's things into his place had the reality of their marriage finally solidified. He'd been worried something would come up to cause a rift.

No matter how often she told him she loved him, no

matter how often he saw the love in her eyes, he still had trouble convincing himself it was real and lasting.

"Wait until you see her in her wedding dress, it'll be worth it," Sean said.

"I know."

For a moment Tanner turned to his friend. Sean had been cheated of his own wedding by Betsy's death. Only now, so many years later, could he relate to the pain and devastation his friend must have gone through, must still feel.

He didn't know how he'd live through the days if something happened to Sunny.

"I appreciate your standing up with me," Tanner said, reaching out to grip Sean's shoulder.

This man had been his friend all his adult life. For the first time Tanner truly appreciated the bond.

Sean smiled.

"What's a friend for if not best man? Ready?"

"Yes."

Standing before the congregation at the huge church that had been Sunny's place of worship since childhood, Tanner watched as the rainbow of bridesmaids walked down the aisle in tempo with the wedding music.

Slowly he smiled.

Sunny had picked an interesting group, Carmella, Julie, Marie, and Ellen. Sean's sister, Gloria, was maid of honor. When the wedding party moved into place, the organ music changed and Tanner looked at the back of the church.

Sunny appeared, holding Theo's arm. Slowly they walked down the aisle.

His heart caught, began beating double time.

She was so radiantly beautiful. And looked as sleek and sophisticated as he could ever have wanted. The dress that had once stood on a mannequin fit her like a dream. The veil that covered to her fingertips didn't hide the shining light of her smile, the sparkle in her blue eyes.

He couldn't look anywhere but at the darling woman who would soon be his wife.

Theo handed her to Tanner, made the proper response and moved to sit in the first pew beside Sunny's mother.

Tanner noticed this peripherally. He was too startled when he realized that she was shorter than normal—barefoot again.

Sophisticated on the outside, his Sunny on the inside. He wouldn't have her any other way.

Linking his hand with hers, linking his heart, they turned to face the minister who would link their lives forever.

If you liked **Finding a Wife For Tanner,**
you'll love book 4 in the Golden Gate Romance Series,
Love Times Three.

If you enjoyed **Finding a Wife For Tanner,**
please consider leaving a review.

More books by Barbara McMahon

Golden Gate Romance Series
Billionaire's Betrothal
Dakota's Hero
Finding a Wife for Tanner
Love Times Three
Unexpected Encounter
Boss's Baby
A Special Kiss

Cowboys of Wildcat Creek
Valentine's Cowboy Rescue
Shelly and the Cowboy
Kristi's Cowboy Hero
Holly's Reluctant Cowboy
A Cowboy for Eliza

Sweet Reunion Romance Collection
Unexpected Reunion
Unpredictable Reunion
Unanticipated Reunion

The Talmadge Sisters
Letters to Caroline
Michelle's Marriage Deal
Trusting Abby

The Harts of Texas Series
Rebel Heart
Tangled Hearts
Reckless Heart

A Sweet Clean Christmas Romance Collection
The Christmas Cop
The Cowboy's Special Christmas
A Soldier's Christmas
A Teaspoon of Mistletoe
The Christmas Locket
A Key West Christmas

Cowboy Heroes Series
Blue Bells on the Hill
Cowboy's Bride
One Stubborn Cowboy
Crazy About a Cowboy
Never Doubt a Cowboy
Cowboy Marshal
Summer Cowboy
Second Chance Cowboy
Movie Star Cowboy

Tropical Escape Series
Island Rendezvous
Come into the Sun
Island Paradise

Rocky Point Series
Rocky Point Legacy
Rocky Point Reunion
Rocky Point Promise
Rocky Point Hero
Rocky Point Inn
Rocky Point Dawn

The Ultimate Billionaires
The Cynical Sheikh
Falling for the Sheikh
A Sheikh of Her Own
The Unforgettable Sheikh

Sweet Romance Stand-alone Collection
Because of You
Cowboy Charade
I'll Take Forever
Jared's Promise
Mail Order Bride
Not Really Married
Sweet Meant To Be
The Cowboy Comes Home
The Paper Marriage
Trusting Jake
The Banished Bride